Can You Keep A Secret?

Matt R. Wright

Front cover photograph by Kevin Nelson
Edited by Ryan O'Hara and Kasey Neth

For Her

1

My story begins well after my 33rd birthday, but still a ways before my 34th. This, I understand, is a very late time for a story to begin, as many stories have already concluded by this time in somebody's life. Unfortunately, I have never been the type of person to be proactive enough to have had a story of my own. Instead I have chosen to live on the fringes of other people's tales. I have drifted through my existence attempting to barely be noticed by anyone other than the few people who remembered my name without my having to remind them. Whenever I would bump into any of the other people at local bars where we had previously met I would watch them struggle as they racked their memory to find my name. Snapping their fingers incessantly, as if the repeating clicks from skin rubbing against skin would jog their memories on how exactly they knew me.

A part of me enjoyed that moment. They make eye contact with me and a glint of recognition flashes across their face as they realize they had met me before in the past, at least once. The glint quickly fades away to a flash of mild terror because they have absolutely no idea when or where they had met me, or what my name is. I get to see that look often when I see people. The bartender who had served me hundreds of beers but had no idea what my name was. I could read at the top of my tab where he had typed the name "Bud Light guy". The pretty girl with the long blonde hair, and slightly too much makeup, who felt we had grown close enough over the course of a night that she and I needed to leave me with a hug, but only referred to me as, "Hey, you," whenever she saw me again after the one encounter. The frat-boyant guy I did shots with and wing-manned for one time when he needed someone, apparently anyone, to talk to the cute redhead with the freckles on her face's friend because the frat boy wasn't dynamic or intelligent enough to entertain them both, but a stand up enough guy to not do as many of his "brothers" did and just roofie the girl. Even the redhead's friend had probably forgotten my name. Not that she really mattered. I don't think I had even caught hers' that night. I was just trying to do a friendly favor for the guy who bought me a shot of Jack Daniels.

I enjoyed being that guy, the forgotten guy. The one guy who people recognized when they saw him but didn't know where they had seen him before. I was one time asked if I had been on television, because a girl with amazing green eyes who I had talked to for an hour and half a week earlier couldn't place where she had seen me. I just smiled at her and told her I was unaware if I had been and continued to walk toward the bar, where the bartender would hand me my Bud Light. I would sit and watch television, getting into a few random conversations with the other drunken barflies who would ask me about the top ten plays on today's SportsCenter and if I knew if the Titans had cut the rookie linebacker who was underperforming in training camp. I would, of course, always know the answer, because a person like me has nothing better to do with his time than watch ESPN and maybe a little of some news station if I could find one I felt didn't swing too far into the left or right direction.

Basically, I never watched the news.

I was a ghost to these people. I could disappear for weeks and come back and nothing would have changed. There would be no welcome banner for me, no groups of people waiting to see me, usually there would be nobody to pick me up from the airport, unless you consider the friendly cab driver from Ghana who had picked me up on more than one occasion. I knew Ekow's name, and Ekow knew where I lived, but he never knew what to call me. He would always say, "Good to see you again, sir," with his Ghanaian accent and drive me home, for which I would tip him exorbitantly because whatever he said to me on the cab ride home was usually the closest thing to a real conversation I had experienced in weeks. I was willing to pay for a good conversation, even if I could barely understand his English due to the thickness of his accent.

When Ekow would drop me off at my little house, in the neighborhood that was just safe enough for a single guy to live by himself, he would wish me luck and tell me to have a great night. Then he would wait for me to walk inside before he would pull away. He was always kind enough to keep his headlights pointed toward the door so I could easily get my keys in the lock without an excessive amount of fumbling, which I tend to do when I can't see exactly where I am attempting to stick the key. Once he would pull away I would watch as the headlight beams moved across my living room wall, up to the ceiling and eventually disappearing, leaving me in a dark room by myself, with a suitcase in one hand and my carry-on over my shoulder.

I would immediately wash any items of clothing that needed to be washed and put away all of my packed toiletries, phone charger, unworn clothing, and any other minor thing I had thrown into my suitcase during packing as to guarantee a fresh start the next time I needed to pack for a trip. I seemed to go on a lot of trips, even though I never really had anywhere I needed to go. One of the joys of being a ghost is the ability to visit many different places without anyone ruining the vacation. If anyone has ever had the experience of taking an unencumbered vacation with no family, no friends, no significant others, to a city where they didn't know a soul, they understand the freedom possessed inside the walls of being invisible.

It is within those walls I lived my life. The ability to disappear on a moments notice with the knowledge that nobody will miss you is a freedom not many people have had the pleasure of experiencing. The lines between reality and the surreal become blurred as I have listened to conversations from the other side of many different bars as I watched the television directly above my head, as well as above the heads of those who are having the conversations. They gab on about their lives, their problems, their dreams, and as I listen to them talk I give them their own lives in my head. Their backstories become fleshed out with every passing moment. I would listen to them talking about how their children aren't getting along with other children in their Montessori school Pre-K classes and I would start to judge them for being bullies when they were in high school. They targeted the defenseless, awkward kid who just wanted to walk safely from class to class without being picked on by the mayor's Neanderthal of a son. Which then added another level to their backstory since their father was suddenly the mayor of some tiny town where nobody actually cared about who the mayor was, except for the Neanderthal son who used it as an excuse to be an asshole. Although, he was probably being an asshole because the mayor was a verbally abusive father who let the Neanderthal son know he would never amount to anything in his eyes. Then I would begin to feel bad for this person whose child couldn't get along with other children in preschool and wish they would be able to stop the cycle before it was passed along to their children. I would find myself forgetting what truths were the ones said by the strangers sitting next to me, and which stories were the ones I created in my head attempting to keep myself entertained as I listened to them drivel on about their children and hearing the boredom drip from their friend's tongues as they droned on about how they understood the dilemmas and wished them luck in their plans for the future. This was the world in which I survived in excess. This was what it was to live in my world.

That was what it was like before I met her.

2

The number of bars I could have been considered a regular of back in those days would have been numerous if anyone would have remembered I frequented their establishments. A few of the bartenders would remember my face and the fact I was a regular drinker of Bud Light. They would have a bottle of it ready when I would sit at their bar and I would either hand them money or they would allow me to start a tab without a credit card since I never walked out on a tab in my life. I never went out to get drunk and forget. I would only have a few beers and observe how real people acted from the periphery. When nobody knows who you are, or even notices you are there, they will talk freely and openly. When I sat at a bar, watching SportsCenter, or whatever game happened to be playing on ESPN, slowly sipping on a bottle of beer, eyes never wavering from the flashing lights of the glowing flat screen propped well above eye level, people would tell me their secrets. Secrets about what they've done. Secrets about with whom they've been sleeping. Secrets about their pasts. Secrets they wouldn't want anybody to know except the person they are confiding in. For some odd reason, that person was normally sitting next to me, close enough that their conversation could be heard as clearly as if they were talking to me personally.

There are so many worlds that exist within a city, and very few of them are not dark worlds. Secrets are the foundation of a world in which lies flourish and trust no longer exists. Possessing the knowledge of these secrets gave me a rush. It was one of the few things in this world that made me feel alive. Upon learning the secrets they were keeping buried from their best friends, their family, their jobs, I could easily begin to make their backstory filled with twists and turns, protagonists, antagonists and, depending on my mood that day, a happy or a sad ending. These stories based on their secrets were more exciting than real life. Real life couldn't live up to the expectations I had set in my mind.

The situation never changed. The words were almost verbatim no matter who it was getting ready to tell their secret. They would be sipping on their drink cautiously. It was always cautiously. Their eyes would shift from side to side to see if anyone was listening. They wouldn't even notice me sitting less than two feet away from them. They would take a deep breath as they worked on building the courage to tell their drunkenly chosen confidant the secret that had been a burden on them since the moment it happened. They would lean in close and lower their voices, but they would be drunk, in a crowded bar, so their natural inclination would be to talk louder than what was necessary. Then they would say the words that made me smile on the inside every time I heard them: "Can you keep a secret?"

It was the sentence of conmen, lawyers, and those who so desperately needed to get something off their chest. Depending on who was asking the question would depend on what the receiver of the question would end up with as a result. They could end up with their life savings in the pocket of a complete stranger. Or their bank accounts saved from the judicial system taking it all since they were able to withhold a key piece of evidence from the knowledge of the courts. More than likely, though, they are being asked to withhold all judgment about a person while listening to a story focused on questionable actions or morals. This is why the asker has to ensure their confidant has the ability to go the rest of their lives without telling another soul, with a simple question that only really has one answer.

There have only been a handful of times, literally, I can count them on the one hand, where the receiver of the secret was honest and said they were not capable of keeping a secret. People love secrets. They love gossip. It's why grocery stores put the tabloid magazines in the checkout lanes. If there is a secret a celebrity is keeping the world wants to know it. They will buy these trash magazines in order to fill their need to learn the dirt on someone else. Is she pregnant? Is he gay? Did he cheat? These are the questions plaguing the minds of the average person as they stand mundanely in line waiting for the cashier to ring up their milk, bread, eggs, and toilet paper. They want to know what other people are hiding. This is why people are forced to lie when they are asked that question.

I'm not sure who initially said it, but the truth of the matter is the only way to keep a secret is to tell one person and then bury them. Someone who is the keeper of a secret, especially one that isn't his or hers, has an uncontrollable desire to tell someone else. They will immediately run off and tell a friend they know they can trust with a secret. Now the number of people who know the secret has tripled in a matter of minutes. The secret is no longer a private contract being held between two people as it spreads like an STD through a close-knit group of swingers. It won't be long before the person who divulged their ever-so-private information is sitting at home, alone, in the dark, waiting for everything to blow over because their secret was discovered by the one person they wished had never found out.

"Yes," the other person says, also loudly due to their intoxication.

"You can't tell anyone," the holder of the secret says.

"I promise."

"Not even your significant other."

"No problem."

That is when they let it out. They get it off their chest. Some act as though they are proud of what they had done. Others act ashamed. Many are just looking for support and an affirmation that they are not the monsters their guilt has convinced them they are in their minds. Once someone tells a friend a secret they are standing in front of them, as if naked for the first time, awaiting the response of the one person they have entrusted with their self-worth at that moment. Doe-eyed, they look toward their confidant, awaiting any sort of evidence they haven't just been adjudicated and negatively convicted in the eyes of a judge they shouldn't have trusted.

Now their secret has nested in my ear as I have calmly been watching the Top Ten of the day and sipping calmly on my beer. This is when their stories begin in my mind. Every detail of their lives fold out in every direction in my head as I create much more exciting lives than any one of them has had the ability to live. Now their lives have had purpose. They have had lives that possessed meaning. They have had just reason to do whatever secret they have accidentally exposed to me.

The tiniest of admissions, such as the ever so common, "I have been seeing a married woman," is all I need to give someone a life.

It starts simply enough, 25 years prior to this moment, give or take a day. He was born to a single mom, whose sperm donor hadn't ever disappeared out of cowardice or fear, but never was given the proper notification he was about to be a father. Due to the lack of both parents in the secret keepers' life he never truly saw the point of long-standing relationships, especially marriage. There was no vow that couldn't be broken. His mother was able to do it on her own, and knowing that guys have the ability to be complete shit if they wanted to, he decided it would be best for him to never find himself in any sort of couple situation in which the girl would think marriage was a definitive conclusion.

This led him into the arms of women who were unavailable for long-term relationships. For a long time he was able to date women who had just gotten out of serious relationships, he was the rock they leaned on until they realized they needed to be on their own. There were many nights after passionate lovemaking with them when they would break down in tears, not wanting to admit to him they had just been thinking about their previous boyfriend, or husband, and not him. He always knew why they were crying, without their admission, and told them it would all be okay. He knew they would break it off soon after and leave thinking they had just hurt him, when in all actuality he had gotten everything he needed emotionally from them already.

As he got older he realized this tactic wouldn't always work. The biological clocks of women began ticking louder and they were looking for "the one". They weren't looking for a short-term rebound relationship anymore. They could move seamlessly from one to the next knowing they were just increasing their odds of finding Mr. Right and not allowing him to slip through the cracks during the in-between times. He also knew he was no Mr. Right for anyone. He had to change his approach, and soon he found he was only seeing women who were already in relationships. Some were just exclusively dating another person. Some were engaged and looking for that last fling before they were tied down. Others were married to emotionally unavailable men. Men who were married to their jobs. Men who were married to their mistresses. Men who were unable to see what was happening.

No, this was not the first time he had divulged this secret to someone. It was only the first time he had divulged this secret to this someone. All he ever wanted was for someone to tell him he was doing something wrong. No one ever did though. They all congratulated him, and told him to keep up the good work. They would inquire about how attractive she was. They wanted to know if she was any good in bed. They wanted to know about the husband. They asked if he was worried about the husband finding out. No one had ever told him it was wrong. So he continued to find new married women. He would start to see them, waiting for the twinge of guilt he felt to build inside of him so he could be justified in telling his secret to a friend he trusted. Hoping that one day he would find someone to tell him to stop.

That day never comes. Instead, in the adult world version of the game of telephone, his secret gets passed along through a plethora of people until it lands in the ears of his most recent conquests' husband. Within a week he would never be seen, or heard from again.

Once I came to that realization I had reached the point where I could finish my beer, pay my tab if I started one, and leave the bar happy to have had found closure on the day.

3

While I was sitting at a bar of which I was a frequenter one night shortly before my 34th birthday I was lucky enough to overhear the secret with which my story begins. It was a secret that many would not have been all that interested in, but the words spoken caught my ear for many different reasons. First of all, this wasn't a secret I was used to hearing. The typical, run of the mill, secrets never changed. How they say there are only a handful of different plot lines, there are only a handful of different secrets in the world. They are as follows:

* Sleeping with someone they shouldn't be
* Committed a crime of some sort
* Have contracted an STD from someone
* Hiding sexuality
* A discovery in their past, which has just come to light
* About to have a child
* Know someone to which any of these are happening

Any other secret is one that doesn't eat upon the soul. It doesn't fester inside of you, itching to get out like a chigger burrowing its way under your skin. The only reason any other secret doesn't matter is that nobody else cares about them. Some may make the argument that telling someone of your addictions is a secret that should be included with that list, but typically by the time the addict is willing to admit his addiction to even himself everybody else already knows about it. Which is why when I was sitting at the bar watching the ESPN Top Ten of the day around the corner from two girls talking to each other it was weird that this secret caught my interest so intently, "I'm going into rehab…"

In all honesty, that wasn't the phrase that really caught my attention. I had heard it uttered many times before in the past and didn't care a little almost every time I heard it. That story isn't fun to make up. It always starts the same way, with the breaking down to peer pressure, usually in the teenage years, and a slow and steady decline into addiction. Rehab becomes inevitable as friends and family now mount a new type of peer pressure on the addict, one where they point out their own wants and desires and make the addict feel bad for wanting his or her own happiness over the happiness of those around them. They break down and go because they cave to the peer pressure, only this time it is to make everyone else happy, which is how they ended up in the predicament they are in now. After a month or two they get out, stay clean for a short period of time, fall off the wagon, and the final, slow descent toward death begins as they realize their lives will never be what other people call "normal." It's a story that isn't ever a fun one to run through my mind, so usually whenever someone tells someone else that particular secret I brush it off as though it isn't possible for that to truly have been a secret. Then I wait for something better to come along. My night can feel fulfilled because I have pieced together someone's life, not from a cookie cutter story that anyone can hear from watching a series of depressing movies or television shows about addiction and the people it hurts on reality channels late at night.

The phrase that caught my attention though was the next

thing that left her mouth, "...for sex addiction."

I sipped my beer and watched on ESPN as a soccer player whose name I didn't know, nor did I care to know, made a goal from what appeared to me to be a reasonable distance. The two mid-twenty hipster kids next to me, who both were wearing glasses that resembled ones I was forced to wear in middle school and was subsequently beaten up for wearing, erupted with excitement at the goal. Then both began talking excitedly about the next World Cup and how unfair it was that America didn't get a chance to host it again, both unaware of the conversation that was occurring only a few feet from them. They continued talking about soccer, pretentiously referring to it as "football" as if we were all living in Europe, but I had already drifted off into the deepest caverns of my mind.

I had never known of anyone with a sex addiction, with the exception of a few celebrity athletes I believed were using it as an excuse for cheating on their significant others. In all my time of being invisible, no one had ever said they were addicted to sex. I had heard cocaine, heroin, alcohol, even meth one time, which is surprising since I was living directly on the "meth-highway," but sex was new to me. I could understand how the drugs could make someone dependent upon them. I knew how after using cocaine people wanted to use more and more until it became debilitating. Even I had experienced mildly similar desires when I was in my early twenties and experimenting with a few college dorm mates. I had never experienced the addiction portion of the drugs though. I never needed them the next day, for which I was eternally grateful. I had also done more drugs than I had sex in my time, so maybe that was what was making it so impossible to comprehend the overwhelming desire just to have sex, to need it the way a heroin addict required a fix.

I sat there in my bar stool, calmly sipping my beer, staring up at the flat-screen TV affixed into the outside brick of the patio bar attempting to come up with a fascinating story to accompany the fact that sitting only a barstool or two away was a young lady who was a sex addict. Every possible story I started ended with my mind racing about how this pathway could have been forged. I began to wonder if I had just been doing it wrong the entire time I had considered myself sexually active. I would never have considered myself inexperienced, but I knew most of the people who had come and gone through my life were probably more experienced than I ever could have considered myself. My mind was spinning with different story possibilities. There was no way I was going to be able to come up with a suitable story for this secret in which I would be happy with the ending as well as the backstory, but I also knew I wouldn't be able to think about anything else for the rest of the night.

I got the attention of the blonde, freckle-faced, bartender with the slight gap in her front teeth and made the international sign for wanting my tab. She brought it to me, thanking me the way she always did for coming in, but never saying my name since she still only knew me as, according to my different tab names I had read, "Bud Light Guy", "ESPN Watcher", or as this nights' read, "Blonde Guy Blue Shirt". I thanked her back, paid my bill and put my grey hoodie on over the same faded blue shirt style I wore every day. I walked inside, to the restroom so I could go to the bathroom before starting my slightly too long of a walk home. While I stood there, staring at the same advertisements I had seen once or twice a week for the past month I continued to attempt to come up with a story suitable for a secret of sex addiction. Every possible theme ended up in a static-filled eruption of failure, as though a storm had just knocked out my television and I never had a chance to find out the ending of whatever I had just been watching. Shaking both my head in frustration and my other head as I finished peeing, I flushed the toilet and watched as the force washed away the inside of the urinal, cleansing it from the piss filled water that was in there only a moment before.

I ran my hands under the faucet in a feeble attempt to be sanitary and wiped them dry on my jeans, which I had now been wearing for a day or two longer than I should have been. I looked at myself in the mirror and felt old for the first time.

I walked out of the bathroom, out toward the front door, grabbing a red and white spiral-colored mint from the hostess stand on my way outside, shoving the mint wrapper into one of the many smoker podiums that littered the front stoops of restaurants all over the city. Sliding my hands in my hoodie's pockets, I started to walk. As I walked, I continued to think. The more I thought about it, the sadder I got. I had begun to feel I had made a mistake along the way. I wasn't sure where I had made the error, but it was growing more and more evident to me that I had no stories of my own. I only possessed and revered the ones I created in my head about strangers I didn't know. I was living in a sad existence, in a tragic world, where the only person I had conversations with was the cab driver who drove me home from the airport on occasion. A block or two of walking had opened my eyes to what I really was; a voyeur of sorts who didn't live in reality, but lived in the stories he made up about others. It was the first time in my life I had realized how pathetic my life had become in the eyes of anyone who knew me, which was nobody.

A car horn honked from beside me. I ignored it, thinking someone's hand must have drunkenly slipped. Again, a short honk rang through the night. I shook my head wondering why anyone would possibly want to honk at me, I was walking on the sidewalk, not along the side of the road.

Another honk occurred, and I turned to look at the car that was honking at me, frustrated, tired and now annoyed.

I looked at the beat-up, blue, two-door that was skulking next to me. The passenger window slowly rolled down. I assumed this was an obvious defect due to the age of the car.

"Hi," the driver said.

I looked inside to see the girl who was sitting a few bar stools away from me at the bar.

"Can you keep a secret?" she asked.

4

I stood there in the chilly Nashville spring night, looking into the window of the blue, two-door sedan idling on the side of the road. I bent over to try to get a better look at the girl who just asked me the question that was the beginning of every poorly decided conversation ever. Her hair was short, shaved on the sides in fact, with a tuft on the top neatly styled and gelled to come swooping down across her forehead and slightly covering her right eye. Her large eyes screamed of sensuality. I could see, even in the dark, she had eyeliner on, which only accentuated the desirability that permeated from her being. They seemed to be looking directly into my eyes, at every single desire I had ever wanted from this world. A playful smirk sat upon her full lips that even as I just glanced at them, I wanted nothing more than to place my lips upon them. I had the feeling they would taste of daylillies. The shirt she was wearing had thin spaghetti sized straps, and I could see a tattoo that appeared to be a vine growing over her left shoulder and a strange circle design on her right arm. I tilted my head slightly and shot her a confused look.

"Well," she said. "Can you?"

I nodded. I had a rock of nerves in my stomach. Everything about this was new to me. I was a forgotten child, one of the great unwashed in this world focused on social media, internet presence and being able to speak louder than the drunk idiot next to you in order to show dominance. Nobody approached me for anything, and while many people had unwittingly entrusted me with their secrets, nobody had ever offered them up voluntarily to me. I chewed nervously on a scar I had on the inside of my lip from an unfortunate accident I had been part of when I was a child. I had adopted the nervous habit when after it had healed and I had discovered it there as my tongue had searched the interior of my mouth for no particular reason one day. The calloused bump crunched quietly as my teeth ground across it.

She smiled at me, apparently charmed by the awkwardness I possessed, not only in that moment but all of my life.

"Get in," she said.

I looked around, confident I was having a prank played on me. This wasn't something that could happen to me. I was not a person who had stories happen to them. I was a person who made up stories for other people. I lived blissfully in a world of mundaneness. The thought of having this girl, this beautiful, mysterious, intriguing woman tell me to get into her car on the side of a road was something I could not fathom ever happening to me. I had never been one to take a chance on anything. Everything in my life had been so cautious, so planned out, so rigid. The man who had woken up that morning would not have gotten into that car, but the man who had realized only a short time ago his life had been an exercise in futility at best had decided to take a chance for the first time ever. With a mildly trembling hand, I reached out and opened the door to her car.

"Come on," she said. "We don't have all night. Well, actually, I guess we kind of do, but hurry up anyway."

I got in the car, shutting the door behind me. Immediately I reached behind me and put on my seatbelt. I looked over at the mystery woman next to me. She smiled at me, chuckling slightly at my apparent nervous reaction to the entire situation.

"I felt you, you know," she said, pulling the gear shift into drive.

I wasn't exactly sure how to respond to her statement. I was unsure of what she saw me doing, or even of when it was she was referring to. She must have seen the confusion on my face and started to chuckle at me once again.

"At the bar," she said. "You were listening in on my conversation with my friend."

I opened my mouth to explain, but was unsure how. I never had to tell someone my secret. I had never told anyone I enjoy going to bars and overhearing other people say things they wouldn't say in a room with only two people, but have no qualms about staying in a room full of strangers. I like to take the information they have shared with anyone who is within earshot and make up a story about them in my mind. How I then like to judge them on the story I had just created about them. No matter how many different ways I ran the scenario through my head, I was unable to find a suitable explanation that wouldn't come off as weird, or creepy, or insane to anyone who wasn't me.

"It's okay," she said. She pulled out a thin pack of cigarettes. They were too small to hold the normal 20 I remembered from my days as a smoker. Slimmer. Longer. Less obvious. If smoking hadn't become such a sign of weakness and the sign of a social pariah, these would be the ones classy women smoked. She pulled one out. Instead of it being white, it was a light brown, with a less noticeable filter than I had seen in the past. The smell of cloves filled the car immediately as she lit it with the pink lighter she cradled in her dainty fingers. "I don't care if you know my secret. In fact, maybe it's better you do."

Again, I looked at her confused. I wasn't sure why it would matter if I knew her secret or not. I was nobody. There were days when I questioned if I was even a real person. Her secret could be nothing less than safe with me. I couldn't tell anyone. I didn't know anyone to tell such a secret. I didn't even know who she was to tell someone her secret.

"I leave tomorrow," she said. "I will be gone for just over a month. All of my friends know where I am going, and why. I can't ask for them to help me out tonight. You, though, are a stranger. You have no connection to me in any way. You and I are going to spend tonight together."

I was slightly taken aback. This woman oozed confidence. She was intimidating in so many ways, from her attitude to her looks. I was unsure of what to do, what to say, how to react.

"It's okay, sweetie," she said. "You will wake up tomorrow and everything about tonight is going to feel like a dream. Just sit back and relax."

I leaned back in my seat and watched the lights pass by my window. Each passing glow of radiating yellowish orange in the night was an opening into a world I had never really been a part of before. I was diving headlong into a sea of uncertainty with the very definition of a complete stranger. I felt alive in a way I hadn't ever expected to feel alive before. Blindly I was entrusting this woman to be my guide into what many would have considered an experience. My heartbeat was rapid. My breath was controlled, but elevated. I felt a little lightheaded from the possibility this night now held. Possibility. I had never looked forward to possibility. I was a man of routine. I had known how and where every night would end for the more considerable portion of my entire life. Since I was an infant. My life had been mapped long before that night had even begun. Tonight was no different until I opened the door of the beat-up, blue, two-door sedan being driven by my mystery woman. She was my Venus in this moment. She was my muse, my Wife of Bath. She was everything I had ever wanted in a woman and I didn't even know her name.

She drove cautiously, methodically through the neighborhood, which was just good enough for a single guy to live in by himself. Her eyes darted from left to right, untrusting of anyone who may have been outside at this late hour. She eyed the speedometer, making sure she wasn't speeding in case a wayward police officer was waiting to pull over anyone who may be on his or her way home after a night of drinking. Just watching her drive I could tell she was cautious about so many things in her life. I wondered why she would have allowed me, a complete stranger, into her car without knowing anything about me. I could have been anybody. I could have a collection of body parts in my freezer I removed with surgical-like precision. She had no way of telling anything about me when she saw me at the bar only a short time ago. I watched her hands grip the steering wheel tightly as her clove cigarette spewed smoke into the car, highlighted by every passing streetlight that still worked as we drove in basic silence. She pulled into my driveway and turned off the engine.

"Tonight," she said, taking a long drag off her cigarette. "I am going to change your world."

5

I watched as this amazing woman slowly walked around my living room, looking at everything I had on the walls, shelves and coffee table. She was meticulously judging me, sizing me up, figuring out how big of a threat I could be to her. She was little. She couldn't have been much more than 5'2" if she even had reached that plateau. She stood next to my bookshelf, looking over the titles of the books I had deemed important enough to keep. Lightly she ran her finger across the bindings of the ones she seemed to have an interest in. Occasionally a slight chuckle would leave her lips as though she was surprised I would own something on display. She didn't know anything about me, but I already felt she knew more than most. She had already gotten farther than anyone else in the last six years or more. Nobody entered my home. It was my sanctuary. It was where I would go and decompress. It was where I thought about my day. I considered all of my daily actions and how I could have made them more streamlined, more efficient. It was where I thought about the people I saw at the bars and what their lives were like with all of their secrets and cover-ups. It is where I could look around and be happy about my choices in life because I knew how all of their days would be ending, and none of them would be as fulfilling as mine. Now she was here and I didn't know what was about to happen. My stomach churned with nervous excitement as I watched her gracefully move through my house. If she had been casing the place, and was planning on robbing me that night, I wouldn't have been mad at her in the slightest. Something about her had a magnetic energy and all I wanted was to find out if her lips actually did taste of daylillies.

"You like the classics, don't you?" she asked, looking away from my bookshelf and back toward me.

I nodded. The classics were the books I had grown up on. Much like some people weren't allowed to listen to modern music, or watch modern television shows, I was only allowed to read books from long before I was born. I was well versed in the old time detective novels, such as Sir Arthur Conan Doyle's Sherlock Holmes. I had read all of Mark Twain. Austen. Steinbeck. Fitzgerald. Bronte. Salinger. Dickens. Hemmingway. I digested those books over and over again. Reading and rereading the yellowed pages, enjoying the smell that burst from each of them as I turned to the next, I learned what storytelling truly was. In those books I learned how someone was supposed to not just live life, but excel at life. I also realized I was too plain and ordinary to ever reach the lofty heights of a character in any of those novels. I didn't have the fortitude to take the chances they did in their lives. I decided at a young age it would be better for me to let them live out their stories, and for me to live vicariously through them by reading of their adventures and imagine how it would feel to be envied by someone like me.

She walked over to me provocatively, stopping only a few short inches away. She looked up at me with her big eyes, her mouth slightly agape as though she was silently begging me to place my lips upon hers. I swallowed nervously; afraid I was going to mess everything up. I caught myself lightly chewing on that scar on the inside of my lip again, as her seductively slightly open mouth transformed to a knowing smirk as in that moment she owned me.

"I make you nervous, don't I?" she asked, her voice filled with an enticing gravel that gave me goosebumps on both of my arms, and the back of my neck.

I nodded. There was something building up inside of me. A force I had never experienced before. I wanted to kiss her, I wanted to taste her lips, I wanted to feel her breath on my face while our tongues danced with each other. The feeling I had in my stomach of nervous excitement was morphing into a ball of courage screaming at me over and over again, "Just kiss her," it yelled. "Just kiss her." It was enough for me to make one move, just a tiny move of my head, leaning ever so slightly to the left and forward. She raised her eyebrows confidently as she knew she had me and reached up and wrapped her hand around the back of my neck, gently pulling my face closer to hers, guiding me toward her lips. I closed my eyes and felt the soft, full, tenderness of her mouth against mine. She didn't taste of daylilies, but instead she tasted of lavender, fragrant, floral, with the slightest hint of mint. They tasted more perfect than I could have ever imagined in any of my overly detailed fantasies.

I could have continued to kiss her all night. The sweet-smelling scent of her breath waved over my face as her hand moved from the back of my neck and she lightly cradled my face with both of her hands, gently biting my bottom lip. I started breathing heavier; a slight sheen of sweat had broken out under my shirt. I was nervous. I wanted everything about this to be perfect, not for me, but for her. She had already created an evening filled with so many emotions I hadn't felt in what seems like an eternity. I wanted to give her the same feelings she had given to me.

She pulled back slightly, and licked her lips, her lavender

tasting lips, looking up at me with the eyes I found myself falling into every time she looked at me.

"Come on," she said, quietly, gravely. Taking me by the hand she led me through my house into my bedroom, seating me down on the edge of my bed, so she was now the taller one out of the two of us. Leaning in, she placed her perfect lips against mine, kissed me while slowly taking off my shirt and tossing it casually to the side. She placed one knee up on one side of me on the bed, then the other flanking me, bestriding me, rubbing her hips against mine. I found it difficult to control my breathing, as I slowly slid my hands under her shirt and slowly, carefully, pulled it up over her head, my eyes never wavering from hers. I tossed it casually in the same vicinity of where she had thrown my shirt, never wanting to look away from her. She was the most beautiful woman I had ever seen, and somehow, someway, I was lucky enough to be with her in this moment.

She reached behind her and skillfully unhooked her bra clasp, slowly taking it off, seeing that I was enjoying each and every moment of this experience as though I was seeing it all for the first time. She continued to rub her hips into mine and I wanted to take my pants off and see what it felt like to be inside of this amazing woman on top of me, but I didn't want any moment she and I were in to end at the same time. Exposing her breasts, she tossed her bra to the side, and even though I tried to hide it, she saw as my eyes light up with excitement like a teenager seeing breasts for the very first time, and her smile grew bigger. She pulled me in close, kissing my lips tightly, her breasts pushed firmly against my bare chest. The feel of her skin against mine was invigorating and sent a relaxed chill down my spine. Her hips pushed tightly against mine and almost involuntarily I began to push mine back into hers.

"Kiss me...here," she said, pointing to her neck, and I did.

Tasting her sweet sweat, that tasted nothing like I would have expected it to, I began to realize how much of life I had missed out on. I wished I had taken more chances. I wished I had more nights like this one. I wished I had been spontaneous. I wished I had actually lived.

"Hey," she said, stopping me from kissing her neck, looking at me directly in the eyes. "I want you to be here, all of you, so stop thinking."

I nodded obediently, she smiled down at me, "Now kiss me here," she said, pointing to her collarbone, and I did. She breathed in deeply, with a slight pause during her inhale as though my lips against her skin had literally taken her breath away. Lightly, she pushed against my chest and I fell back, landing into my sheets. She motioned for me to move backwards onto the bed. I scooted back until we were both lying in bed together, skin tightly pressed against each other, lips tangled with passion, our breath getting more and more rapid, as she slowly took off my pants, while I slowly took off hers. Her teeth bit my lip and she would occasionally let out a delicate moan. I wanted her so badly. I wanted to be one with her. I wanted to know what it felt like to be in her. I wanted it all so much it was almost impossible to slow the rocking of my hips into hers.

Gently she took my hands and placed them up above my head, where my mattress met the wall and held them there, not forcefully, not dangerously, but caring, softly.

"Pretend they're glued there," she whispered in my ear, lightly biting on my earlobe, and kissing my neck. She took her hand, reached down and slid me into her. I lost my breath as I entered and my first instinct was to move my hands and hold her tightly to me. She held my hands where they were, and continued to grind her hips into mine. "Shhh, they're glued there. You can't move them."

She then sat up and slowly rocked back and forth, looking

at me, directly in the eyes. Her breasts playfully bounced upon her chest and her hands pushed against my hips as she masterfully maneuvered up and down. With every downward motion we would both have to inhale deeply to keep from passing out, as the moment of nervousness and uncertainty had evolved to a moment of beauty and passion. In this moment I felt alive, I felt what I had read on all of the pages of all of the books I owned, I felt the excitement and the rush of being human I gave to every person I made up stories for at the bars. I never wanted the moment to end as I watched the beautiful woman's face on top of me experience a pleasure I had never witnessed ever before in my life. In a moment of unbridled joy and with a mutually uninhibited desire to be everything in the world for the other person in my bed that night I experienced pure and utter contentment as I saw her face as she had the most beautiful orgasm I had ever been fortunate enough to witness.

Lying there in the dark, moments after, her head tucked gently in the crook created by my shoulder and chest, with my hand lightly dragging across her back and arms I could have died without much care for anything else in the world. My legs were numb, my back was covered with sweat, and I had a smile on my face that couldn't have been removed with the most untimely of news. I understood happiness for that brief moment, and wanted so much more of it in my life. I wanted what this woman had given me. This glorious gift was the most precious thing I had ever received, and I already feared I would never see her again.

Not long after, she sat up and started to gather her things. I wanted to stop her, but I had no idea what to say. I couldn't tell her not to go. We had only just met. I couldn't keep her here with me. I could only hold on to her memory, and the events of tonight as I moved forward with my life. She looked at me and smiled. She reached into her purse and pulled out a pen and a pad of paper.

"I have a rule," she said. "I don't stay over at boys' houses. Especially since I am going to rehab tomorrow. But write your number down, and maybe, when I get out, I can send you a text and we can get coffee."

I took the pen and paper and scribbled down my number for her. She took them from me and placed them back in her purse. She kissed me with her lavender flavored lips and inhaled deeply as she pulled away.

"Dream about me tonight," she said, walking out of my room. I jumped out of bed, naked, wanting to stop her from going, to beg her to stay, but she had already gotten to the front door and was gone before I could say a word to her.

6

She was gone. I had no idea where she had gone; only that she had gone to rehab. I didn't know where someone would go to rehab for sex addiction. In my wildest imaginative dreams I couldn't picture what an acceptable facility for this kind of addiction would look like, only Orwellian style institutions of sadness and despair. It seemed to me as though other people wouldn't be able to be around, as the temptation to sleep with someone else would be too great for other people suffering from the same malady. I envisioned separate rooms with padded walls, away from anyone or anything that could be considered stimulating. The only people you would see on any given day would be the person who drops off your food, and your therapist who would be helping you get to the root of your addiction. All outdoor time would be equally separated between the other members of the rehab clinic, carefully, cautiously constructed so no client would ever see another member of the clinic. The fear of people relapsing while they were under the care of the clinic would be too great. Lots of time would be spent by oneself, taking the time to remember the good things in life, trying not to focus on the bad memories, but to see the good possessed in small pockets of the world. Which when attempting to be victorious over an addiction of any sort is usually a task that is almost as inconceivable as the notion of getting through the day without getting off in some fashion.

She and I had only spent one night together, but I had felt a connection with her I had never felt with anyone before. I found myself sitting in the darkness, staring out a window towards a blank canvas of nothing thinking about her. I would listen to the repeating drone of the fan spinning above my head, wanting to fix it so it would stop making the annoying noise, but too depressed to do anything about it, wondering where she was. Trying to picture what she was doing at that moment. They were lonely nights, like most of my nights already were. These were different, though. They were plagued by an emptiness that rested somewhere within my chest which had the most mild sensation of burning. My throat would feel as though it was about to close from time to time. A high pitched ringing would hang out beside my eardrum, slowly pushing me closer and closer to the edge of madness as I begged for it to stop. I would spend time weeping. Tears would flow from the ducts as I would struggle for breath, eventually finding short gratification when I was able to inhale a lung full of oxygen accompanying a wailing groan, which echoed in my brain and reminded me of how alone I had become in my time on earth. I was unable to do any work. It seemed as though I had lost all control of my faculties. The only thing I was able to do on a regular basis was masturbate while I thought about her, and the night she and I spent together. I would picture her perfect face, and her beautiful blue eyes. I would think about how she told me to kiss her, and where to kiss her. I would taste her on my lips and smell the mixture of lavender and cloves wafting like a ghost through my house. I would remember what it felt like to be in her, not just physically, but how it made me feel to be inside of her and how I never had felt like that with anyone I had ever been with before. I would picture her face, and the look she had in the moment I was able to bring her to climax. That would be when I would reach climax with myself every time. Four times a day, without fail I would remember that face.

The moment I would finish I would look at my life, what I had become, wondering why anyone would ever want to talk to me, eventually realizing nobody ever did talk to me, except her. This would be when I would start to sob again, which I was only able to stop eventually by pleasuring myself again while picturing her face. This was my lifecycle for what seemed like months of loneliness I had never experienced before. I had no need to go to bars and watch ESPN. I didn't care about top plays. I cared about her. I wanted her to be safe. I wanted her to be healed. I wanted her to be out of rehab. I wanted her to be here, with me. I wanted her.

I couldn't contact her. I didn't have her number. I didn't know where she was. I would close my eyes tight and try to imagine a scenario in which she was living a happy life. I would see her in a white T-shirt, too big for her frame, covered in paint. She would be sitting on the floor, working on an art project of some sort. Painting pictures of a life where whatever had caused her addiction and sadness didn't exist. She would be smiling, laughing. Her eyes would have a glint of real life in them. There wouldn't be the sadness that rested over them like a glaucoma-induced film hiding the beautiful luster that inspired poems of Homer-esque proportion. Or I would see her smiling peacefully as she played with a little kitten in her bed, playfully pushing it away then pulling it back towards her. Squeezing it in a gentle hug, burying her face in its mussed fur and kissing its little face. I tried to picture a life in which she and I would be doing these things. A life where she and I were together, living in a world where I wasn't alone, a world where she was happy and free. Those fantasies never played out though and eventually in a haze I would see all of the terrible endings our life would endure, each one worse than the one I envisioned before. A series of events that pulled my heart out of my chest, threw it on the floor, ending with me alone on my couch masturbating to thoughts of her, and her in rehab somewhere because she had relapsed and couldn't function anymore. Both of us alone, forever trapped with the memories of each other. Perhaps it was better we only had that one night.

I would try to convince myself of this as I lay on my couch staring at the spinning ceiling fan in virtual silence. The sounds of the high-pitched whine and droning ceiling fan, the only noises to be heard. I would lie to myself and say she was just another girl. A girl I would soon forget. She had already forgotten me. It was only one night. She'll be gone from the memory bank soon enough. There will be another girl soon. She wasn't even real. I made it all up. Among many other stories I would concoct in order to try to deny she and I had a connection that was anything short of undeniable. My heart would beat rapidly when I thought about her and my body would break out in small amounts of sweat. I felt tired all the time. I felt like I had lived a pointless life. I cursed her for making me realize that, but then would apologize to her specter a breath later for cursing her. I felt confused. Conflicted. I hated her. I loved her. I hated myself for loving her only after the short night she and I had spent together. I wished I had a healthy way of releasing my anger, but I had nothing. I wasn't good at sports. I couldn't punch hard enough to dent drywall. I had no desire to drink. I just wanted to sit in the darkness and think about her. A sharp enough razor wouldn't be able to end anything successfully. My future was going to be filled with many nights alone with my thoughts, tears, and box of Kleenex.

For weeks upon weeks this was my life. I would go through this day after day. I wanted her back in my life. Staring at my phone I would wish it to ring. I would hope she would see that slip of paper I wrote my number down on and she would call it, just to say hello. Just so I could hear her voice. Just so I could know she was real and I didn't make up the entire evening. After six long weeks of self-pity masked in self-gratification, followed by self-loathing, I decided it was time for me to go out and find her.

7

I had all but lost my complete desire to go to bars. The act of sitting in public, alone, drinking while watching ESPN had lost all of its luster since I spent that night with her. She had shown me something of beauty; something a night wasted in a bar would never be able to match. If I was going to start looking for this beautiful angel I would have to do it outside of local bars. I wasn't even sure if a recovering sex addict was allowed to drink. If someone was an alcoholic they could still have sex, but it would probably behoove them to stay away from drugs and bars. I would imagine a sex addict was the same way. I remembered sitting in all of the bars observing as drunk girls and drunk guys would embarrassingly flirt and paw on each other, leading to the inevitable moment the next day when she would be walking from the cab she took from his house to her car, heels in hand, makeup smudged, shameful and self-loathing. He would brag to his friends about his conquests and talk down about her in veiled attempts at making himself feel better about the fact he hated himself for who he had become. He was nothing more than a frightened little boy with no self-control and cripplingly low self-esteem. He knew he did what he did because he was afraid his friends would make fun of him more than they already did. He hated it when they called him names, especially when they used the word, "Fag," because deep in his heart he knew it was true. To avoid the degradation, he slept with woman after woman with no regard to what he was doing to their self-esteem, their bodies, or himself. Because of people like this, people like him, I didn't feel she would feel comfortable going to bars to hang out. Now I had no purpose to go to bars at all.

I found myself constantly in poorly-lit church basements or gymnasiums, waiting for the moment where I would once again see her face. I would sit and listen while the meetings would go on. I would hear the stories of the people talking about how long it had been since they last were with someone. They talked about how much of a struggle it was to get through the day-to-day life without being tempted to just take someone home. It didn't matter who that person was, either. They just needed to be with someone. Their need to feel desired by another human being was the strongest desire they had. As I listened to them tell their stories about how degrading their lives had become before they realized they had a problem, how their problem had developed, and the damage it had caused, I began to think about my own life. I started to question everything about my daily routine. Spending the entire day going through the cycle of self-gratification I had found myself in as of late was right on the edge of compulsory behavior. Like an alcoholic can't stop himself from drinking, I was now incapable of going a single day without pleasuring myself while I thought of her. Typically it was happening multiple times, with the frequency ranging depending on how much water I had drank the day before. I wondered if it was possible that due to my desire to see her again I had stumbled into the groups that would be able to help me with my masturbatory problems.

Day after day I found myself in a different church basement hearing stories I was completely unable to comprehend the basis of. All of the urban legends were false. There were much worse things going on in this world than what we heard in grade school. They would tell their tales of bottoming out while always having the glorious moment at the end where they would raise their arms triumphantly while exclaiming how long it had been since they last had obligatory relations with someone else. This number could be as low as a week, or even a day, while others were celebrating their achievement of years, showing off their chips they received for passing these milestones. The look of accomplishment beamed from their faces as they walked from the podium and all the others clapped to show their approval for what they had done. They all would rejoice with their mantra "You Are Not Alone," and I would always applaud along, like the laugh track to a sitcom or a talk show, wondering how it would feel to achieve such a thing. I couldn't go an hour without thinking about her. How these people were able to go years without stumbling was a mystery to me. I honestly thought they would be filled with a type of sadness, which some were at times, but more often than not they were filled with hope. They made me wish I understood what it was like to be hopeful. I envied them at times.

Weeks passed. I had been attending any meeting I was allowed to attend. I feared she was going to meetings that were exclusive to women, or ones requiring prescriptions from therapists or doctors. I started to recognize people, not by their names, but by their stories. They were also starting to recognize me, even though I never spoke at the meetings. I would get the knowing glance as I walked past the group of smokers in the entryway to the church. As I walked down the fluorescently lit hallways I would receive the nods of recognition one gives to an acquaintance or someone they recognize but they aren't really sure from where they would know each other. Occasionally someone would say "Hi," or "Hey," but it never went much farther than that. I felt like a fraud, one which was on the verge of being discovered if anyone were to ask me a question about my problems. I had considered attempting to play mute as my reason for never speaking but feared someone would know sign language and want to communicate with me. I knew I was visiting on borrowed time. They would soon find me out and my attempts at finding her again would be for naught.

I sat down in my metal folding chair with the hard plastic seat and waited for the meeting to begin. The smell of stale coffee hung in the air as it did in every meeting I had attended. Addicts and bad coffee, the two were always abreast. I stared off into the distance, chewing on my lower lip, hoping I was still able to give off the impression I was not someone who was ready to open up. I had to avoid conversations for as long as possible. I knew I would soon have to disappear from all of the meetings. They would find out I wasn't going to therapy with anyone. They would realize I wasn't addicted to sex, or love, or relationships. In fact, I had spent the better portion of my adult life without any combination of those three things. They would see me for what I was beginning to see myself as, an obsessed man with a schoolboy crush on the girl who gave him the adult version of her pudding cup at lunch. Maybe it was time for me to leave. Time to give up my quest. I started to stand when I felt the touch of someone's hand on my shoulder and the smell of stale coffee suddenly dissipated, and in its place was the combination of the heavenly scents of cloves and lavender.

I turned quickly to see her standing behind me, wearing a blue sleeveless hoodie, with the hood up, a loose-fitting black t-shirt, shorts, and look of knowing and confusion as to why I would be sitting in one of the rooms she had been frequenting for weeks now.

"I wasn't sure if I would see you again," she said, as I slowly slid back into my uncomfortable chair.

She walked around and sat down next to me. I was somewhat afraid she would be mad at me for seeking her out the way that I had, but her smile led me to believe she was fine with my attendance at the meeting.

"It's good to see you again," she said, her blue eyes sparkled from the now flickering fluorescent light bulbs above.

I smiled and chewed on my lower lip, trying not to show her how truly excited I was to have finally found her, what seemed like months later.

8

She took me to a coffee shop after the meeting. Luckily, Nashville had many coffee shops that remained open until the late hours of the night, or the early hours of the morning for late night workers, college students studying, or the derelicts of society to sit in and evaluate where their lives had gone wrong. She and I were in none of these groups. We were two people who were finding each other, connecting, in the dark back room of a coffee shop away from the eyes of the general public as though we were hiding a secret affair, after leaving the dark dingy basement of a church listening to people tell their stories of woe. The stories of how these poor people only felt any positivity about their lives when they were having sex. It didn't matter with whom they were sleeping with either. It could have been men, women, friends, people who were in relationships, people who were in relationships with the sex addicts' friends, people who were in relationships with the sex addicts' family members. They didn't care.

They hated when people called them "sluts," or "whores". They hated these words because deep in their hearts they knew they were true. And that knowledge is what hurt them the most. They knew they were addicts. In the eyes of the world they were the lowest of the low because they didn't care who they hurt in their uncontrollable selfish attempts to feel better about themselves. They wanted the ever-lost upon them feeling of self-worth they experienced whenever they knew they could seduce someone into bed with them, although, the moment they were finished they knew they had only hurt one more person. They were leaving a wake of people with broken hearts in addition to the series of people who would never trust them again. They all congratulated each other on their individual accomplishments; making it one month without having sex, making it two. Soon, they would break and have to give back the ever so coveted chips they earned by doing something I had found so easy to accomplish, until she came into my life.

"You were looking for me," she said, as she sipped her raspberry macchiato. "Why?"

I shrugged. I knew the answer to that question, but I didn't know how to truly express it to her. How can one tell a sex addict he had been looking for her because she had completely blown him away during sex? I couldn't tell her how all I had been thinking about was her, and how she made me feel for the first time in my life as though I wasn't invisible. I couldn't explain how no longer did I long to hear people's secrets so I could make up their backstories and fill out their fictional lives with unbelievable details that could potentially never happen to anyone, and then judge them for the stories I made up about them based on one little secret they admitted to the world. We had only known each other for the one night, and I couldn't express how in that one night she had changed my world. I couldn't even discern if she had changed my world for the better or for the worse. I couldn't figure out how after just one night with her, I had become addicted to her. It was more than just an addiction. In someway I had fallen in love with her that night. I would assume it was part of her charm. It was probably one of those qualities that had led her down the path that resulted with her involvement with sex addicts anonymous, or as they called it SLAA, sex and love addicts anonymous. In the same way the heroin user needs the second fix after his or her first injection, I needed her in the same way I had her what seemed like months prior to this night.

"You understand I am an addict," she said, staring sultrily at me from somewhere behind her blue eyes. "An addict with many other issues, besides being just an addict."

I nodded. I did understand. I wouldn't be able to feel her touch on me again, but just to be in her presence was like a methadone injection, calming my innermost desires to be near her, around her, in her. I longed to kiss her lavender flavored lips. I wanted to feel her soft skin against mine still, and hear her raspy voice whisper in my ear as she asked for permission to cum. I knew, though, I had to digress and not give in to my desires, because I also had a uncontrollable inclination to keep her safe from any harm that could confront her in this world. I didn't know where this paternal instinct had come from, but I knew I wanted to keep her safe from anything, and everything in this world.

"You would never do anything to hurt me," she said, sipping her fruit-flavored beverage. "Would you?"

I shook my head, and took a long sip from my non-fat mocha. The feel of the warm chocolate espresso as it slid down my throat and the warmth of it penetrating my stomach, relaxed some of the tension I had been feeling in the conversation she and I had been sharing.

She leaned back in her chair, little wisps of her hair stuck out so carefully from underneath her grey stocking cap. She knew they drew attention to her eyes. She knew her eyes were where her seduction was the strongest. She knew I wanted to reach across the table and place my hand gently against her face, and slowly guide it towards mine, feeling my heart rate increase as our lips would move closer together and soon I would taste her lavender flavored lips. She could see in my eyes I was playing this all out in my head, and a smirk crossed her lips as the realization of my addiction to her became apparent to a person who understood everything about addiction.

"You really wouldn't," she said. "But trust me when I say I am going to hurt you."

I nervously chewed the scar on the inside of my lip as I watched her smirk slowly fade away, now replaced with a stone-faced look of sorrow. She shook her head, looking at me in a condescending way, as though I was a child who was unable to care for himself and needed someone to look after me. She was slowly deciding she was the one who was going to take care of me.

"You're too nice of a guy," she said, grabbing her purse and standing up. "I don't want to hurt you, it wouldn't be right."

I reached out and gently grabbed her arm. I wanted to be careful not to scare her, or make her think I would ever do anything to force her to do anything she wouldn't want to do in any way. I wanted to protect her from everything in this world, even if that meant putting myself in harms way, to protect her from herself. She looked down at my hand gently resting on her arm, and an affectionate smile crossed her face. Her eyes, closed for a moment as though she was savoring the feel of another human's touch against her perfect skin. She opened her eyes and looked down at me. I motioned for her to sit down, and she did. She understood I was a grown man and could take care of myself. I didn't need anyone to look after me, just as she didn't need anyone to look after her.

"I have a lot going on," she said. "I can't be in a relationship. This can be nothing more than a simple friendship."

I shrugged again. I didn't care in what facet she and I shared each other in our lives; I just knew I wanted her to be in mine. Her addictive quality had grabbed hold of me in the middle of my chest and held on tight. Being around her in this manner had already relieved some of the pressure I had been walking around with for days. She sat back down and gently took my hand in hers. A rush was sent through my body as her fingers became interwoven with mine, and our bodies had become tangled together again, in a much less biblical way this time, but still a way in which I could truly feel alive again.

9

Friendship. It always seems like such a good idea whenever you are talking to someone you want in your life. Let's be friends. We can be friends. We can never be anything more than just friends. Friends are good. Friends are necessary. You can judge a man by the quality of his friends. A person without friends is the loneliest of people. These are all lies. Just like every other lie we tell ourselves in order to make it through the nights of being overly needy and anxious about what tomorrow will bring. The days when you wake up and you can't seem to shake the fog that rests in-between your ears. The mornings where you can't jump-start your brain into working properly, because someone or something else is residing in the temporal lobe and won't let go until you talk about it with a friend. This is when we say we need friends and we reach out to anyone who will listen to our problems and issues, when in all honesty we probably just need to sit back, meditate, and work on the issue in the head instead of relying on nights of self-abuse, and gratification, mornings of sloth-like activity, and days upon days of binge drinking until we have finally forgotten the person or thing that has made us a shell of the people we used to be. The loneliest person in the world isn't the man with no friends; it is the man who is in love with someone with whom he cannot be.

She and I wouldn't talk or hang out. We would breathe each other in. She would ask me questions about my dreams and my desires for my future in this world. I would ask her about what she wanted to do with her life and how she was going to get there. The simple basic conversations you have with people as you slowly get to know them. These are the conversations that are supposed to build up to relationships. These are the conversations that supersede falling in love with someone. Not for me though. No, these are the conversations I have with the woman I had already fallen in love with. Filled with a desire to be with her, I struggled through the mundane activities of basic friendship while the whole time staring into her eyes, knowing that at no point in the history of my existence had I ever felt anything like this for anyone who wasn't a fictional character. She was so much more than Daisy Buchanan, or Elizabeth Bennett, or even Helen of Troy for that matter. She was something I wouldn't just imagine in my head over and over again, creating a world in which she doesn't end up with Mr. Darcy, but instead runs away with me to a tropical island where we would trade wit-filled banter while discussing the current issues and the proper ways to repair relations between feuding nations. I could see just by looking at her that she was less self-involved than Daisy could ever be, and while her face could launch a fleet of ships, she never would have allowed a war to break out over her absence. Although, if a war had broken out she would be filled with the same self-loathing over the incident. What she had was something I had come to regard as a mystical like quality, a quality so many other people had taken for granted and abused throughout history. I was able to see this quality for what it was, and was able to hang on to it with all I had. She had the wonderful quality of being real, and that was something I had never had the pleasure of truly realizing in anyone before her.

It is in seeing the realness of a person where one truly can fall in love. In a world of plasticity where no one, or nothing is what it seems you can relish in the triumph of finding someone who acts like him or herself around you. It is within the lack of these barriers where true acceptance is found. It was within these walls I was able to act and react with her, and it is within these walls she was able to act with me. While I had already fallen in love with her, I assumed it was in the confines of our relationship that she, too, was falling in love with me. The wayward glances, the flashes of desire, the conversations about what a future between us would possibly look like if she ever were ready to be in a relationship again were all signs pointing me in the direction that this girl was the girl who was not only going to be the girl who would show me what it was like to love, but was also the girl I would spend the rest of my natural life with, and if there was such a thing as an afterlife, I could only hope I would spend that time with her as well.

On occasion she and I would begin to show each other exactly how much we cared about one another physically. Our lips would meet and the passion would dance between the two mouths, begging for us to go farther than we knew we were allowed to proceed. As her hand would slowly start to massage my already erect penis, I would have to do the, unfortunately, chivalrous thing and tell her it was time to go our separate ways, because I was never wanting to be the one who caused a relapse, nor did I ever want her to blame me for anything that ever would, or could, go wrong in her life. These nights were often followed by nights where she would call me and tell me she so very much wanted to see my body, naked, next to hers. She would begin to tell me all of the things I would do to her, if it was her choice, and even though I could never prove it, I always imagined her masturbating while she told me these things. Then she would hang up the phone, and I knew I wouldn't see her that night, and possibly the next, even though I would think about her before I fell asleep, and when I woke up the next morning.

So the nights in which she would disappear because she warned me of how dangerously close we were getting to having her break her streak of sobriety, I would have to wonder who was out there in the night, while I stayed at home watching mindless television shows that had little to no bearing on my life as it stands today. The nights were dark and lonely. They were filled with thoughts of a sex addict fighting through a craving the way a junkie attempted to overcome a bought of withdrawals. There was no methadone clinic to help ease the desire to have sex, it was a battle an addict must deal with every day, every night, and in moments of jealousy filled rage I would wonder if tonight was the night she would break down and relapse with someone who wasn't me. These were the thoughts of the loneliest man on the planet. Not the man without any friends whose only thoughts are those of what comes on ESPN next, or what sort of sad dinner for one he will be having. The constant worry that the woman you love is out there picking up a random stranger at a gas station to fuck in the dingy, small, disease-filled bathroom so she can feel some shred of self-worth instead of just coming to your house to sleep with someone who truly loves and cares about her is the most crippling thought a person can have. This was a thought I had often, and it was on the brink of driving me mad.

Unfortunately there was nothing I could do about it though. I couldn't tell her how I felt about her, because I would then lose her. I couldn't tell her I wanted more than what she and I had, because I would lose her. I couldn't end the relationship because I had become dependent upon our time together. If I were to ever lose her I knew I would regress into a man I never wanted to, or thought I would, become; a man with an incurable emptiness in his chest. A man who could barely come up with the strength to get out of bed. Living his days watching entire streaming seasons of television shows on his phone without speaking to the outside world. I knew mine would be a sad existence without her in my life. So I refused to ruin that by telling her I wanted more than a friendship, living in a world of my own silent pain. I was to play the role of the supportive friend who was there for her whenever she was feeling weak. I would never be allowed to capitalize on these feelings though, because with the burden of unconditional love, comes the responsibility to respect and protect her from any and all evils, even if I was that evil. Instead I would sit at home clinging to my cell phone as though it held all of the answers to life, the universe and everything. Waiting for a phone call or a text message letting me know that my only friend, but not my girlfriend, was okay. I slowly started to despise my life. Not because I missed my old one of creating fictional worlds for the strangers next to me at bars, but because I felt as though I was living in a world I had created for a stranger, and I couldn't turn it off. There was no ending in sight for my story, and the long string of pain and loneliness I would feel due to the fact I had fallen in love wasn't going to get any easier in my eyes.

10

"What's on your mind?" she would ask me, coyly peering at me with her blue eyes. There were so "What's on your mind?" she would ask me, coyly peering at me with her blue eyes. There were so many questions hiding within the sporadic green and gold flecks that gave her eyes a special quality. One which I could never find a proper descriptor. Beautiful? Too generic. Magical? Too fantastical. Unbelievable? Not believable. Amazing? Inspiring? Life-affirming? No. No. No. There was something about them that could not be put into words, at least not any words I knew. I would stare into them whenever she asked me a question and wonder what it was she really wanted to know. It was never the question at the surface that required the answer, it was always a question two or three deep that she wanted the answer to. It was as though she was asking a question for a friend of a friend. A "My friend wants to know if you think she's cute," kind of query. It was difficult to say who the actual person wondering these types of things was, and while she was the only friend I had, and I, for all intents and purposes, was the only person she ever saw, there never was any real comfort in the idea she was the one who actually wanted the response.

I would smile and look to the side, never really answering

any question that seemed to be more rhetorical than it was genuine. There was no purpose in destroying the dynamic of a relationship which up to that point and beyond had been completely devoid of small talk and plastic veneer conversations. It didn't matter what the weather was like recently, or what happened on whatever TV show was popular at the time. All that mattered was how close she and I had become in such a short period of time. I couldn't really remember how long she and I had known each other, nor how long it had been since the two of us had last shared a bed, but I knew it hadn't been that long. While it also seemed to have possessed the same amount of time as the rest of my life. She knew my feelings on the shallow and meaningless conversation. There was no purpose to it in life, except to kill time while surrounded by people one found to be wholly characterless and obtuse. I found her to be neither of these things and would like to think she found me to be quite the opposite of them as well.

"Did I ever tell you I was adopted?" she asked.

I wondered for a moment who would ever want to give this wonderfully sweet person away. She was so adorable now, in her mid-twenties. I could only imagine what she would have been like as a child. So full of energy. Exploding with life. Waiting for night to pass so she could greet each day with a smile and hope for a better one than the day before. Giggling about the simple things. A butterfly flitting about the yard. A breeze blowing dandelion seed heads in the springtime. Then I realized if her birth parents hadn't given her up in hopes of her having a better life, then she and I wouldn't be where we were at that moment. She wouldn't look at me as her best friend, and I wouldn't be in love with mine. Instead, I would be sitting at a bar, wearing the same style blue shirt I always wore, watching SportsCenter, and drinking Bud Light, as opposed to sitting on the couch at her house while watching episodes of old TV shows we both had seen more times than we could count.

"My parents adopted me when I was two," she said. "I don't really remember anything before that, of course, I mean, who does? But I sometimes wish I had a memory of my birth parents, just so I could understand why someone would ever want to give their child away."

I understood that. I never really saw myself as the fatherly type, but parts of me wanted to know what could possess someone to bring life to this creature, made of two peoples' DNA in the act of passion and togetherness, and then just pass them off to someone else who wasn't ever lucky enough to have the joy of conceiving and birthing their own child. If I believed in God I would imagine there was a reason those two people weren't supposed to have a child, and therein is the reason he cursed them with the unfortunate burden of being barren. It seems as though anyone who believed in God enough not to abort a child, should also believe in his or her infinite wisdom enough not to allow couples to have a child they could not produce themselves. I guess that's why people tell that other lie to themselves whenever something bad happens in life, "God moves in mysterious ways," or the even bigger cop out, "God has a plan." Either way, I knew if I were ever to father a child, I would be there for that child's life, attempting to care for it as well, if not better than my father could for me.

"You know I have a lot of secrets, right?" she asked me. She appeared to be searching for my validation, which I would always give to her, as long as she needed it. I didn't care about pasts, and secrets and mistakes people lived with, because unlike the people who used to tell me the lies about God, I believed in forgiveness. Whatever happened before we met, and anything that happens after we part ways, fell into a category that I considered none of my business. There are decisions everyone makes in life, and while everyone likes to say they don't have regrets, it's another lie we tell others to make us feel better about the secrets we share with random strangers in bars, late at night, while searching for validation, just like she was at this moment. I would never judge her, nor would I ever say a cross word about her. I was the safe spot. In her life filled with paths and trails of darkness and danger, I was the nightlight letting her know the monster lurking in the corner was nothing more than a coat hanging on the back of a chair. I would be the one person who would never break her, or anyone else's, heart.

I lightly grazed my hand across her soft cheek, and smiled. I gave her the reassuring look I had seen in movies, on television, and in bar after bar time after time. The look stating I was there, I was listening, and I cared about what was bothering her, while not caring about whatever was bothering her at the same time. I was there to be with her, unconditionally, until the end. It didn't matter what secrets were being buried deep inside her conscious. There was something about unconditionally I understood for the first time in my life. We may not have been sharing a bed anymore, not since that first time, but that wouldn't have mattered anyway. My love for her was deeper than physical. It was as though I was a part of her, and she was a part of me. It may have taken me the better part of 34 years to find someone I could feel close to in any way, shape, or form, but I was lucky enough to find someone I felt connected to emotionally, physically, and spiritually. A lifetime of loneliness had found reprieve. I had wasted night after night in bar after bar listening, ingesting, caring about stories I made up in my head, while all I was really searching for was someone with whom I could write my own story.

Secrets meant nothing anymore. They were little aspects of the world that had no bearing on anything real. I didn't care what her secrets were. They were of no consequence. As long as I could spend time with her, whatever secrets she held close to her chest, would hopefully find way to redemption, or at least to a point where she was comfortable enough talking about them with me.

11

Learning more about her past made me wonder about my past. I started to worry about what in my history would be considered weird, or odd, in the eyes of people who may have grown up with normal, or quintessential lives. I may not have had a lot to brag about my childhood, but I also didn't have anything to complain about. She had been adopted, and while a part of her seemed to be ashamed of that fact, there was a bigger part of her that seemed to revel in it. Why shouldn't she though? At the age of two she had more of a story intertwined in her life than I had at 33. She was already instilled with a sense of mystery and intrigue, backstory and plot line already in place, before she was even capable of creating a memory. My backstory was nothing more than a lifetime of forgotten memories and repressed darkness I attempted to forget while drifting my way through a life of mundaneness. In seeing the incredible life she was able to live, while dealing with every terrible issue she was faced with, I was able to see how sad of an existence I had been living. I wished I had been able to tell people stories about my past. I wish I had one memory that was worth bragging about to anyone who would be willing to listen. I never had the guts to attempt to anything fun, or exciting. I never drove across country because I was in love with a girl. I never drunkenly got married in a bar on my 30th birthday. I never partied in Atlanta with a Swedish rock band while they were on tour in America. I never went to a wedding, much less got into a fight with the groom's sister's date at one. I wanted just one story to tell people at parties, assuming I would ever get invited to one in my lifetime, and then feel comfortable talking to people who were also in attendance. I wished I could be something more than the supporting character in the story where I was intended to be in a staring role.

At my age though I had already succumbed to the idea that I would always be a background character. I didn't mind that fate most days, in fact I appreciated the ability to blend into the scenery. It allowed me the ability to hear all of the dirty secrets this town had to offer, and to create a world in which I was not a supporting player in it, but the creator of everyone and everything. The way I had dedicated living my life could have even been considered more sane than any other way, since I was in control of every single variable that would come along. The only thing that had altered my reality was her inclusion into it. Once she had entered the realm of reality I chose to live in I was unable to discern what was made up in my mind, versus the world that everyone else seemed to truly exist in. The story I had been attempting to live my entire life, while pushing myself into the darkest depths of the background, was suddenly lacking in excitement. There were moments I despised her for ruining the reality of my world, but I was in love with her, which made me glad I was able to destroy the walls of my reality in order to see what things such as feelings, and emotions were really like.

As she lay there, with her head nuzzled in my shoulder as the television blared loud, innocuous noises while flashing brightly colored lights that made little sense to me I could see the brilliance in everything she was, and I could feel how I desired to be like her in almost every way. I also wanted to fix her in every way while not changing her in any way. She was a paradox in my mind, in my heart, and in my soul. I would be amiss if I were to ever lose her, not only for losing her, but also for losing the life I had spent 33, almost 34 years building, or not building depending on how one were to look at it.

12

"A few of my friends are going out tonight," she said. "I think it has been long enough."

It had been months since either of us had done anything besides sit at the house and watch television. The most we would do was go to meetings in order to help her avoid having compulsive sex with people, despite the adverse consequences these actions may have. Once we would leave a meeting, we would head back to the house, and sit there on the couch next to each other, talking about the meeting and all the good it was doing for not only her, but for me as well, while the television blared at us. The longer we talked about the meeting, the more she would begin to think about sex, and then she would want to have sex...with me. She was never sure if this was a genuine feeling, or a compulsive one, so we never would, but instead we would find another meeting to go to, and we would leave the confines and safety of my house to visit another dank, dark, church basement where people would be describing their desires of having sex with random strangers, teachers, police officers, grocery store baggers, fast food workers, friends, or even family members when the time was dire, or when their story was even more dire. We had fallen into a vicious cycle of complacency, which I was accustomed to but she, on the other hand, had never fallen victim to a life of normalcy and routine so she was not equipped to handle the mundaneness of a regular schedule.

"While I love being around you," she said. "I need to get out of the house for something other than a meeting. I need to go out and dance, and have fun, and just get rid of all of this pent up energy I have welling up inside of me before it all explodes and I do something I regret, and blame you for."

I was not a fan of the idea of her leaving to go out for a night with her friends and going to a bar to dance with all of the negative influences the world possessed, but I also knew she was not someone I would ever be able to keep from doing whatever it was she wanted. Not that I would ever want to keep her from doing anything she wanted, or hold her back in any way, I just want her to be safe and protected, and while I knew her being around me was not always the best way to make sure these things happened, I was almost positive the situation she was willingly putting herself into was more dangerous than being around me at the house.

She looked at me with her blue eyes, and I could tell she saw the concern I was feeling. She reached up and gently placed her soft hand on my cheek, lightly rubbing her thumb back and forth, soothingly. Her touch eased my concern, but I knew it was only a patch worked solution. The moment she was gone and out there, among the evil that populated this world, with all of the temptation and distrust that fed the greater mass of society, I would once again begin to worry about her safety and well-being. I would wonder if I would ever see her again. I would wonder if she would remember me after she was gone. I would wonder if I was even worth remembering, the way I would always remember her.

"Don't worry," she said, in a soothing voice. "Everything is going to be just fine. I am going to be coming back to you very soon, and we will hopefully be able to spend the night together sometime in the near future."

It was with those words my life had been revived with the worst punishment the creator had ever doled out to humans...hope. Hope always felt like a great thing. Hope allowed someone the ability to believe, but more often than not they were left wanting with nothing more than hope for tomorrow to appease their pain. It was the equivalent of every single religious person across the globe who hoped their religion was the correct one, or even more accurate, they hoped that if their religion wasn't the correct one, then none of them were so they wouldn't be punished for believing in a false deity, or for participating in the shameless acts of hating others because of their beliefs, sexual orientation, skin color, or nose size. In the eyes of the religious they hope they are right, or everyone, including themselves, is wrong so they won't be forced to live an eternity of punishment they always thought was nothing more than a stupid fairy tale. This is where she had just left me, hoping beyond all hope that she and I would be able to spend another night together soon, and if not soon, eventually, and if not eventually, at some point in the ever-expanding future.

I sat in the background as I watched her get ready for her big night out. With every careful brush of her hair I worried about what her night was going to bring, but if it was just another step on her road to recovery, and another step on the road so she and I being able to actually be together in a way where all parties were invested in an emotional and physical relationship. Every stroke of her eyeliner left me mute, while I anticipated her leaving only so she could return again to me, slightly more healed, and ready for a nurturing and healthy relationship. Whatever worries I possessed I held close to my chest. I didn't want her to see me as over possessive, or needy, although I was exactly those things. I wanted so many things in life, and almost all them had to do with her. Every ounce of happiness I could have possibly envisioned was centered on her. I could worry day in and day out about what may happen when I wasn't there, but I figured if she never saw my concern she would go on assuming I was more than a caring, trusting, good-natured person. Each outfit she tried on I saw as one less outfit she would have to try on before she and I would finally be able to be together, for the rest of our natural lives. And as she walked out the door all I could hope for was this would be the last time she would walk out the door where she and I weren't together.

13

I was awakened the next morning by my phone ringing loudly ripping me from a dream in which she and I had been out together, drinking and dancing together, surrounded by some of her friends and a lot of strangers. She and I were in the midst of hundreds of people, but still completely alone together as we held each other close, swaying to the beat of the music. Enveloped in darkness, with only the strobing colors from the many different neons, and electronically choreographed lights to illuminate her face, she and I stared into each other's eyes, feeding, internally on the soul of the person in front of us. The person we were in love with. The person with which we saw something more than a one night stand, or even less; a quickie in the bathroom. There she was in my presence, just as I was in hers, a person with whom I could see a future, based on a mutual disdain for anything mundane and ordinary while being completely complacent in our lives together. In my dream I was content, overjoyed, and happy for the first time I could remember in my entire life.

I answered the phone to hear her crying, sobbing, begging me to meet her at a coffee shop by our respective houses so we could talk. I was worried but knew I had to be there for her in a time where it appeared as though she needed me to be there with her the way I would imagine a real boyfriend would be there for his real girlfriend, even in a time of strife. Surprisingly, for me, I wanted to be there for her though. I had always thought I was more of a person who just wanted to be around people during their good times. At a point when they were already on the mend, or when they had been fixed by someone who was a professional.

She looked at me with understanding in her blue eyes. It was almost as though she knew exactly what I had been thinking, what I had been stressing about, what I needed from her to let me know I wasn't just another nobody who she would one day forget. She could see I needed to understand her pain, and with that, I would be better at understanding her. I tried to reach out again, this time attempting to caress her cheek lightly, but again she pulled away from me, so I retracted my hand feeling rejected and hurt that she couldn't, or wouldn't, trust me. She looked again at the adjacent wall, and then silently at the floor. She closed her eyes and coughed. It was a light cough, not the type of cough one would expect from a smoker, but instead the cough of someone clearing their throat.

Sitting there, across from the girl I was in love with, I watched as something strange happened. It wasn't something that could easily be explained, but she transformed in front of me. Her appearance changed, ever so slightly, but still so very noticeably. Her face appeared thinner, mainly in the cheeks, taking away from the chipmunk essence she possessed normally. Her hair seemed to get thicker, with more body and slightly lighter in color. Her mouth shifted and now rested in a different position than how it normally rested. She opened her eyes and looked at me. Staring back at me were confused eyes with little recognition behind them. It was as though the person looking at me had never seen me before, and I wasn't entirely sure I had had ever seen them before either.

I looked into the confused now emerald green eyes staring back at me. They appeared to be slightly lost and unsure about where they were. There was no fear behind them, as though they had experienced this sort of thing before. They darted around the room quickly, gaining the bearings of the room. She reached out and grabbed her coffee and took a long sip. Her face turned to one of disgust as she swallowed the coffee and she shook her head, putting the drink back down on the table and pushing it away from her as though she had tried it for the first time in her life. She looked across the table at me, and a smile crossed her face.

"Hi," she said.

Her voice was different. It had a higher pitch to it, and just in the one word, I could hear the youthfulness that danced in the octaves of the tones. I was taken aback. All I could think to do was say hi back and wait to see what was going to happen next. She looked at me with a childlike grin plastered across her face. She seemed naive. Youthful. Playful. Happy in a strange way.

"How old are you?" she asked me.

I looked at her, confused by the question. She knew how old I was. We had discussed that before. She even had made fun of me for the age difference between us.

"How old are you?" she asked again, slightly upset that I hadn't answered her yet.

I told her I was 33, not quite 34. She looked at me with the same amount of disgust she looked at the coffee with.

"You're old," she said, placing a lot of the emphases on the last word as opposed to the first. "What are you doing with her?"

I had no idea who she was talking about. Who was she referring to? She was the only person I had spoken to all day. Why was she suddenly so offended by my age? It had never come up in conversation before. She didn't seem to care if I was in my thirties and she was in her twenties until today.

"Do you want to hurt her?" she asked.

I asked her who she was referring to and the green eyes of the girl in front of me grew wide with surprise.

"Oh," she said. "You don't know. I shouldn't have told you. I'm sorry. Don't tell her. She'll get mad at me if she knows I told you."

I sat back in my chair. My mouth sat agape. I had no idea what was happening. Part of me thought she had lost her mind, part of me thought she was fucking with me in order to push me away. I wasn't sure if I should walk away, or if I should talk to her more, to try snap her out of whatever was wrong with her. I asked her what I wasn't supposed to know. Sadness came over her. Her smile faded and morphed into a frown.

"She didn't want you to know yet," she said. "She thought it would scare you away."

I leaned forward, reaching out and grabbing her hands gently. She pulled her hands away quickly. I could see she was looking at me as though I was a stranger, not someone who could be trusted without time. I looked her in the eyes and assured her I wasn't going anywhere.

"There are lots of us," she said.

I shook my head. I wasn't sure what she was referring to exactly.

"She has lots of us," she said again.

I asked her who she was talking about and the girl in front of me sighed, exacerbated by my ignorance. She pulled her hands away from mine and shook her head.

"Her," she said as though I should know exactly who 'Her' was, and still understand everything that was occurring at the moment. "She has lots of us."

I sat there, utterly bewildered by the conversation I was

having at the moment. I had no idea what to say. Everything I said ended up circling back to an answer that only confused me more. Annoyed, tired and confused I asked her how old she was since she was acting like a petulant child.

"Silly," she said. "I'm Twelve."

I leaned forward, gazing into the green eyes of the girl staring back at me. I saw it then. I wasn't talking to the woman I loved. No, I was talking to someone else. I was talking to a child. I was talking to a 12-year old girl who was living inside of her body.

"I mean, I'm almost 13," she said. "My birthday is in two months."

I wondered how long she had been saying that sentence. Obviously, she hadn't aged in many years. I wasn't quite sure how multiple personalities worked, but I didn't think they were born like people and aged in time in a linear sort of way. I was pretty sure they just were. They never grew older, or matured, or changed in any way, outside of the trauma they experienced due to the horrible things they learned while staying the same age, or as in this case, being stuck at the age of 12 for well over a decade.

"School's been really hard this month," Twelve said. She had visibly become sad as she said these words. I could see the stress of being 12 and all of the pressure that comes along with it painted on her face. I remembered all of the peer pressure that occurred when I was in grade school, and I wouldn't ever want to relive those moments. Unfortunately for Twelve, it was all she would ever be able to experience, and as I realized this, my heart broke for her. "All of the girls in my class are mad at me. I did something bad."

She looked upset as she thought about it more. I told her it was okay and it whatever happened didn't matter. There wasn't much that could happen that would hang with you for life, so whatever was bothering her couldn't have been that bad.

"You really think so?" she asked.

I nodded, showing her my sincerity about the issue. I could barely remember any experience that shaped the person I had become while I was in school, so I was pretty confident in my answer.

"Good," she said, a wave of relief washed across her face. "I was worried that the girls would stay mad at me for sucking on Christine Fagler's boyfriend's penis in the bathroom for a long time."

I looked at her with shock and surprise. I couldn't believe that a 12-year old had to deal with issues and worries such as that. I hadn't ever had the drama that came with the random hookups. I had once seen a stand-up comedian who said that every girl has a dick they regretted, and every guy had a pussy they regretted. I never understood the joke, because my insufficient amount of physical relationships I had, I never regretted any of them, although every time I thought of that joke I wondered if I was the one the girls I had experienced physical relationships with regret.

"He ended up telling all of his friends about what I did for him," Twelve went on to say. She looked sad and somewhat distant. "So all of them wanted me to do it for them too. And I wanted to be liked, so I did it, and then their girlfriends all got mad at me. One of them wrote 'whore' on my jacket in permanent marker. My parents got really angry about that. It was an expensive jacket."

I watched as Twelve fiddled with the napkin in front of her. Her little hands tore pieces off and rolled them into little balls and just dropped them on the table, causing a small-scale version of the Milky Way to form around the coffee cup. I started to look for constellations to form, but I was unfortunately never creative enough to see the constellations when I had a map of the stars in front of me, I definitely wasn't able to see any I made up in my own head. With each ball that fell to the table, all I could see was a bigger mess someone was going to have to clean up, and not a mythical being who had a great story on how he ended up living out the rest of eternity in the tiny universe of random discarded trash.

"You're nice," she said. "I don't even feel like you want to hurt her. Not like the others. You seem like you care about her. A lot more than others have. A lot more than the guy she woke up next to today."

My heart simultaneously sank and rose into my throat at the same time. I had a pit in my stomach and a lump in my throat that was making it difficult to breathe. Quickly I understood why she had called me and asked me to meet her today. She needed to tell me that she had gone home with someone. Some guy she met last night. Some guy whose name she may not have known. Some guy who hadn't been there for her night after night. Some guy who hadn't attended meetings whenever she felt obligated to have sex with someone. Some guy who was out at the bar, who had a car, a shiny shirt, a personality, and the ability to talk to a girl. He was probably thinking he was being slick and had a lot of moves, but all he was doing was harming all of the progress she had made over the past few months.

Twelve's eyes grew wide as she saw the realization come across my face that she had spent the night, romantically, with someone else. Tears began to well up, and her lip started to quiver. She shook her head back and forth quickly.

"No. No. No," she said. "Don't be mad. I'm sorry. I'm sorry. Don't be mad."

The more she spoke, the worse it felt to be me. I was watching as the heart of a 12-year old was breaking in front of me, because she thought she had done something to hurt me, while I wanted to be mad at the person whose body she happened to be currently residing.

"Don't be mad at me," she begged. "I thought you knew. I thought she told you already. I'm sorry. I don't want you to be mad at me. I know she really likes you, and I don't want you to be mad at me."

I didn't know what I was supposed to do. Was it okay to get up and just walk away from the table, or would that be essentially leaving a preteen alone in a public place? I was looking at the face of the woman I loved, but into the eyes of a child who wanted nothing more than to make everything better and didn't want me too mad at her for something she had absolutely zero control over.

"Please, please, please," she went on to say. "I'll do anything for you if you won't be mad at me. I'll even do for you what I did for the others if it'll make you happy. I just don't want you to be mad."

I was at a loss for words. I had wanted more to happen between she and I for so long, but something about this seemed so...wrong. I wouldn't be having sex with the woman I was in love with, I would be having sex with a childish version of her, and that would probably cause more damage to someone was already so broken I may cause her to never be able to be repaired. I shook my head and told her I didn't think it would be a good idea when her eyes went vacant, lifeless, and dark. She closed her eyes, and for a second it appeared as though she had fallen asleep. A few light coughs left her mouth while her eyes were closed, and when she opened them the emerald irises that had previously been there were back to the beautiful blue eyes, I had fallen in love with what seemed like months before. She looked around nervously, anxiously. She saw the look on my face and immediately knew something had happened.

"Oh no," she said. "Who did you just meet, and what did they say?"

14

"I found out about them when I was 18," she said. Her face was a mix of emotions. Part of her seemed ashamed of her situation, while another part of her seemed to embrace it with the confidence and bravado I had come to fall in love with over our time together. "At first I thought I was a freak, I was convinced nobody would ever love me because I had these other versions of me living inside of me."

I could understand why she would think that. The world was filled with those who didn't accept what they didn't understand. Even the so-called tolerant ones were filled with prejudices and hatred they attempted not to show to the people they deemed important. They would judge someone wearing a button down and a tie as a right-wing fascist as quickly as a member of the KKK would accuse a person with a dark complexion of being from a lesser bloodline. In their inner circles they would talk down and insult the people they thought were ruining the world, but they, themselves, were too weak to actually do anything about it. These were the people who would look upon her, not as an equal but, as someone who they would want to observe and get to know as part of a social experiment so they would be able to tell people about their friend with multiple personalities. They probably also told people how many black friends they had when defending themselves against anyone who would have the gall to accuse them as racist.

"Part of the problem is people don't understand what it is," she said. "They call it things like multiple personality disorder, which isn't what it is. It's called Dissociative Identity Disorder, and it just means there are..."

She shook her head while she sat there, staring at the constellations of ripped up napkins in front of her. I didn't know how many people she had tried to explain this to, but I was pretty sure it was never an easy situation to have people understand.

"Imagine your body as a small bus," she said. "And you are the driver of this bus. You may have other people in the bus with you, but they just sit there silently, watching the scenery as it passes by. On occasion, the other passengers in my bus decide they want to drive, or sometimes I subconsciously decide they need to drive for a while, and they take over the wheel."

She picked up her cup of what now had to be a cold raspberry macchiato and sort of fumbled with the cup, not ever drinking from it, nor putting it back down. She just held it as though it was her safety blanket. The only protection between her secrets and me was a small cylindrical piece of recycled cardboard.

"There are a few of them," she said. "There are five, that I know of. You met Twelve, of course. There's Six, Sixteen, Nineteen, and Thirty-Three. They all have their own distinct personalities. They come in at different times. Sometimes it's because they think I need to be protected from people, or myself. It could be because I'm remembering things."

Her eyes filled with tears. Memories were attacking her brain, reminding her of every bit of hurt she had experienced over the course of her life.

"Sometimes it's like the stuff that Twelve told you about," she smiled slightly as a slight bit of reprieve came from remembering, and the faintest of laughs escaped. "I can't believe she fucking told you about John. Did she offer to sleep with you?"

She looked at me for the first time since she had realized what had happened. Her blue eyes shined brightly, accentuated due to the thin veil of tears that rested on her lower eyelids. I could see the fear the Twelve had asked me to sleep with her, and how she was unsure of the answer I would have given. I nodded and lowered my eyes, ashamed.

I wasn't sure why I was ashamed, I hadn't said yes to the offer. It may have been because I hadn't had a chance to answer before Twelve had left and even though I knew my answer would have been no, I would never prove it to her, or myself.

"Sorry," she said. "Twelve will do that from time to time, but you can't ever say yes. It is basically the same thing as agreeing to sleep with a minor. You can do serious damage."

As she explained the rules of being around someone with dissociative identity disorder, I felt myself feeling a little hurt. I had been a guy who hadn't pressured her into having sex with me, even though I knew I would have been able to convince her it was the right thing to do, by preying on her weaknesses and addictions. I never wanted to be that guy with her, and the insinuation I would take advantage of a 12-year old, albeit a 12-year old living inside the body of a 25-year old, showed a sense of distrust I didn't appreciate her holding of me.

"Sixteen," she said, her voice trailing off for a while. "I don't know how to say this to you. I don't want you to be upset."

I can't imagine how finding out about anything else would upset me more than discovering the girl I was in love with had put herself into a position where she was unable to stay strong and slept with someone else. Then learning she had multiple identities living inside of her. Then being propositioned by one that wasn't even a teenager yet. There were things I could imagine upsetting me in this world, but nothing could upset me more than I was at this moment.

"Well," she continued. "Sixteen likes to seduce people, and I have little to no control when it happens. She has a compulsive desire to have sex, especially with strangers."

This must have been how she ended up going home with someone last night. She found herself in a situation she was not equipped to handle, and one of the others had taken over the driving of the bus. Sixteen had taken the wheel and had driven her right into the arms, and bed, of a man who they didn't know and probably would never see again. She was trying to find a way to tell me about what had happened, and her nervousness came across as cute, only because I already knew the problem, and I could see she was working hard to protect my feelings.

"The night when we first slept together," she said, her eyes welling up with tears again. "That wasn't me. That was Sixteen. She was in control that night. I had nothing to do with what transpired between us."

My heart sank. I felt weakened throughout my soul. The night I had considered to be one of the greatest of my life, and had been my only sexual experience I wanted to cherish and remember, had been the result of a dissociated break, and while I thought I was falling for the woman who sat in front of me now, I had actually been falling for a 16-year old version of her. I had fallen for this woman, while she didn't have a recollection of what had gone on. I had just been another nameless individual who had been a result of a bad childhood, and a potentially worse adulthood. I was certain if I let her explain more she would have a lot to say, and convince me that she was truly sorry. Knowing me, I would forgive her and give her another chance, but nothing about my world was real anymore. I had never experienced a love this great, and now I learned its foundation had been built on a lie. The feeling of my heart shattering inside my chest was almost unbearable. It hurt for me to look her in the eye, at her mouth, at her hands, at her at all. I shook my head, clenched my fists as not to show her the pain I was feeling inside, stood up from the table and walked away.

I could hear her crying, but I didn't know if there was anything she could say to make any of this better, or normal. Instead, it was time for me to walk away and work on getting my life back to the normalcy of solitude and loneliness where I couldn't be hurt by anyone, especially her.

15

The last time she and I stopped seeing each other, it was because she had gone to rehab. She had up and disappeared from my life in order to better herself. It was apparent, though, that even through all of her time in the rehab center she was still a ball of problems. Problems that couldn't be solved by a caring ear, open heart, or anything else I could offer her, but problems that were reliant upon real psychiatric help. Help I was incapable of. Help she didn't seem to want to get. She had subconsciously created a world where other people would be there to handle her problems for her, a world where she may not have to deal with the minor issue that was bothering her in the present, but one day would have to deal with a much larger and severe problem. While I spent my days reveling in my loneliness and embracing the fact I didn't have anybody by my side, she had gone off in the opposite direction with it. I had spent a lifetime growing accustomed to being alone. I had been training myself to be ready for this moment. This time there would not be days lost to self-loathing, depression, and self-gratification. This time it would just be me living my life of loneliness. There was no need to search the world for someone I had placed on a pedestal after one night of gratification. Now I had taken the time to get to know someone, and based on the information I had gathered from getting to truly understand how someone thinks and acts I could safely walk away without ever thinking about her again.

This was the lie I told myself every morning as I woke up and started my day. I would sit in the darkness of my room, waiting for the earliest semblances of sunlight to peek through my blinds, thinking to myself how today was going to be the day where I would finally stop thinking about her. She wasn't important to my life, or to anyone's life except for her own. Whatever she had going on in her world had no effect on my world, and while I knew this to be a true statement whenever I would think it, I would wish I knew how she was, where she was, what she was doing, and with whom, all before the sun would finish rising. Then I would get out of bed and shower in the darkness, not because of my crippling depression, but because for some unknown reason my lights would never work before 9:00 a.m.

I would stand in the shower as the almost flesh burning water would cascade down through my hair, down my body, onto the tiled floor and down the drain, where it would disappear from my life forever. I found a slight enjoyment watching the water draining out of my life. There was a finality to it that gave me comfort. Some things were final. They were going to be gone for the rest of my life, and that thought made me happy. That thought meant I had no control when things or people would leave me, that was just the way the world spun, and as it spun in that way, I would continue to lose things, and people, and that was okay because that's what was supposed to happen.

I slowly understood I was not a person who was supposed to have a story, no matter what my overactive imagination had been telling me as of late. I was a person who was a part of a story, someone else's story. I was a side note, a footnote, a

Cliff's Note, but not even worthy of my own book. I would stand there in the shower and think about my eulogy. I would think about my funeral, and then I would think about the eulogy. I would think about how I would die, then the funeral, and then I would think about the eulogy. While the way that I would die, and the place and number in attendance would change, the eulogy would always remain the same. It would be spoken by the pastor, or civil servant, or whatever poor soul was charged with overseeing my funeral with anywhere between zero and nine people in attendance, of which she was never one. This unfortunate person who would be the master of ceremonies of the saddest funeral to ever be performed, which I hoped would one day become my claim to any sort of notoriety in anyone's eyes, would look out among those, if any, in attendance and say:

"While he may have existed, he never truly lived."

It was always then that I looked at my razor sitting on the wire shelf in my shower and contemplated how long it would take for anyone to notice my body if I had just slit my wrists, making sure to cut the right one first, since my left was so much weaker than my right. Would it be long after I had stopped paying my rent that someone would come to show the house and find my body? Would the water from the shower still be pouring over my lifeless form, which by that point would have morphed into a unique gelatinous mass of a leftover body, and nothing all at the same time? I would run the blade over my wrists, but the only thing I had the courage to cut was the baby fine hair that nobody would ever have seen any way that grew in the spots I fantasized about slicing into.

I would finish my shower just before I would get the courage to slice my skin open allowing my blood to pour out and down the drain with the water, adding to the things I would never see again in my life. Then I would brush my teeth, and immediately drink coffee, because as my nights lasted well into the early hours of the morning, the sleep I had never allowed me to sleep past the early hours of the morning. I was continually working on three hours of sleep, and I would continue to tell myself I was happy, and I was content in my life. Lukewarm coffee, stale bagels, long showers, and minimal hours of sleep was enough to keep me alive, unlike my life with her. She was a destroyer. She worked toward bringing people down. She was a negative force in the world, and even though I was completely and inexplicably in love with her, I was afraid of what would happen if I would ever see her again. The reason being that no matter how bad I knew she was for my life I wanted her in my life and I was almost certain I would put up with just about anything in order to be with her.

I would sit on the couch, stare at the television and wonder where I had gone wrong. Was there a moment in my life where I had gone wrong or had I been traveling down this path since I was born? Was I fated to be the nothing I had become or had I chosen that path? Life seemed to be a constant montage of kicks to the testicles as I was constantly reminded that I was the equivalent of nothing when it came to life. I would pass away one day, forgotten by anyone who at one point knew my name, and the only thing left on this world to remind anyone of me would be a modest tombstone that would eventually be overgrown by weeds and flowers that lazy, underpaid, uncaring groundskeepers allowed to disappear into the oblivion of headstones of the great unwashed. I would think about my inevitable demise and look forward to the day I would take my last breath, so I could be placed into the earth and finally give something back to the world that hadn't given me anything, but I still felt as though I owed it something. I apparently continually felt indebted to those who did absolutely nothing for me, except fuck me when I was down.

16

I had stopped going to meetings. I didn't want to find her. She could go to whatever meeting she wanted to go to without the threat of me being there to confront her about my problems with her. I was working on being content sitting at my house watching television by myself, drinking beers while I waited for my pizza or Chinese food to be delivered. I didn't want to feel as though I needed to be attached to her anymore. I wanted to get away from the feeling that I needed someone else around me in order to feel whole. I wanted to find that feeling within myself. I had absolutely no idea how or where to find it, but I wanted that feeling. For the first time in my existence, I wanted to be more than just a fragment of a person. The only issue I had was I had no idea on how to become more than a shell of a person. It was all I had ever truly been.

I decided returning to old patterns would be the best plan to get back to who I used to be. Once I got back to the place I used to be, I would be able to work on myself and get to a where I was not only independent from all people but also a functioning and normal member of society. It was all reliant on finding the person I had been months ago, before I met her before she came into my life before one of her other selves had shown me what it was to feel again. I wanted to be the lone soldier in a battle that was completely nonexistent to the rest of the world. Like most battles being fought by lone soldiers, my battle was internal and wouldn't be noticed or cared about by anyone other than myself. Those, though, are the toughest battles to wage, and even tougher to win, as I was certain many other people in the world had realized long before I had made my decision to alter my existence for the better.

That night I was going to go back to one of the bars I had frequented in the past, and I would sit there, drinking my Bud Light, and watching SportsCenter until I heard a secret that would allow me to create a back story on an individual I had never met, or had even seen before. I didn't care if it took me until the last call, which I had never actually been present for before, I was going to hear the secret that would allow me to begin the process of becoming a normal human being. A part of me, a part I had never realized existed before, started to swell with excitement at the idea of working towards being a better and more normal person. I was suddenly filled with a warming sensation that grew from my center and began to permeate outward, extending toward the limbs and appendages filling them with feeling. A slight tingle began to dance on my fingertips, and I understood for the first time what it was to hope for something that may not actually be achievable. Living a safe and untouchable life was easy and organic. There was nothing dangerous about how I had been living until I met her, and now I had the chance to live a life where risks were involved. It was as though I had been reborn. This was probably the same sort of phenomenon religious people experienced when they allowed Jesus into their heart or life, or whatever it was they did in order to feel better about all of the darkness and pain in the world.

I flipped through the channels with my remote, nondiscriminately. I had no idea what I was passing up, nor did I comprehend what my eyes were seeing. All I was considering was the night. I began to fantasize about what secrets I could possibly hear. I wasn't being greedy. I didn't want to have a bombshell sort of night where someone was admitting to the time they hit someone with their car and just kept driving or anything. I would have been okay with an easy affair, or a closet case. Even someone admitting they had a problem with self-mutilation would have been okay with me. I just wanted something, anything, that could get my mind working in the way that it used to.

I leaned back farther on the couch, resting my head back against the cushion. My mind danced with the possibilities of what may happen later that night. The sounds of the television slowly blurred into one monotonous sound that tickled my eardrums the way rain hitting a tin roof, or waves crashing into the shoreline might soothe people to sleep. My eyelids grew heavy as the constant white noise of random channels flipped across the screen. My thumb continued to press the channel up button, as with each passing station I could feel myself fading farther and farther away from the land of the awake, and into a world where I was no longer intimidated by people I did not know, but instead was a type A personality, or even an outgoing type B, who had absolutely no qualms with approaching strangers in order to make general and pleasant conversation. My thumb grew weaker, and eventually, I stopped pressing the channel up button as my eyes closed, and I drifted off.

17

That night, wearing the same blue, v-neck, T-shirt I often wore when I was out at bars in the past I went to one of the many bars I could have been considered a regular to see if I could find a secret I could expound upon for the first time in more months than I could recall. I walked past the hostess, who had long brown hair, and matching eyes. She was dressed all in black, but not in a gothic, or punk sort of way. She looked classy, with her porcelain skin, and carefully maintained lipstick. She was the classic definition of beauty, and while I wished I could find a way just to say hello to her, I was certain she was not any sort of person who would be interested in me. No, I understood what I was in this world. I was one of the forgotten, and she was one of the ones who would always be remembered. Throughout time and torment, nothing would phase her beauty. She would be the lucky woman who kept her looks after birthing multiple children, and as she got older, she would become more exquisite, exuding class and brilliance as she gained notoriety for being special. She was not a girl who would look twice upon me. To her I was invisible, and I was accepting of that fact. She didn't even look up when I passed by her to go to the bar. I received no acknowledgment whatsoever, not even a smile, or feigned "hello" when the door opened. This was the reason I would never speak to a girl like her; she was too well put together ever to see someone as broken as I was.

I weaved my way through the small sea of people who were meandering around the bar area with no real destination in mind. They didn't know if they should wait for a table to order anything, order drinks from the bar, or purchase something from the tired looking server who had grown weary of pushing them to the side every time she had to make her way from one side of the restaurant to the other. This was the group of people every server undoubtedly hated seeing. They took up space, didn't spend enough money to make their existence worth putting up with, and acted as though the servers were a bother when they were attempting to nothing more than their jobs. I hated them, and that was just from my time dealing with them in bars and restaurants I had visited. They lacked a certain amount of what I had always considered common courtesy and looked down their noses at anyone who wasn't them because of how much they secretly hated their lives.

Making my way through the cocktail area, I reached the exit to the outdoor bar, where I was certain the blonde girl with the cute gap in her teeth would be working. The last time I had been at this bar I had met the woman I fell in love with. I was hoping this time I would be able to change my life again. While I didn't really believe in fate, karma, destiny, or a god who had an unwavering and uncontrollable plan for everyone on earth, I hoped that lightning could actually strike twice. Maybe, just possibly, if I were able to sit in the spot where my story had started, I would be able to find the next chapter before my story came to a disappointing and forgettable conclusion.

I sat on the corner stool, on the side that allowed me an unimpeded view of the television, which fortunately already had SportsCenter showing above the beer taps. I settled into my old seat, grabbed a beverage napkin from the napkin holder, neatly placed it in front of me, and waited patiently for the bartender to come out. After a couple of the top plays were shown, neither of which impressed me all that significantly, the blonde bartender came through the plastic wind curtains that seemed to be more of an impediment than anything else when carrying multiple drinks, or a tray of any kind.

She walked over to me with her smile, flaunting the genuine beauty possessed within her gap. While some people would have considered something like that a character flaw, or a problem, she seemed to be the type of person who embraced it as something that made her unique and special. Her great smile was only shadowed by the sparkle of life she had in her eyes. They were an icy blue that reminded me of a frozen lake, where the sun would shine down, melting portions, allowing for the darker blue waters to break through, giving hope for warmer days to come.

"What can I get ya?" she asked, and a part of me felt a little rejected. I had hoped she would have remembered my order, but I also understood this was a large request, as she never even asked my name, and it had been months since I had last shown up at her bar.

I told her I would like a Bud Light, and she nodded, flashing me the same beautiful smile she showed every customer she hoped would reward her with a generous, and potentially hefty, tip. She walked away, disappearing back through the plastic curtains, while I waited patiently for my beer.

I looked around the bar, hoping someone would jump out at me as someone who may be the possessor of a great secret. A secret I would be lucky enough to hear and then, allowing my mind to take control of their story, I would become free again.

To my left were a few hipsters, both of them, in their quest to show their individuality, were wearing flannel shirts that were slightly too tight on them, dark jeans, that were exceptionally too tight on them, black Chuck Taylor's, and thick-rimmed glasses that I would have wagered were for decoration only. Their hair was the only difference about them, even though it was evident that both of them had spent an exceptionally long time attempting to make it look like they had spent no time at all on it. One was long on top, parted to the side, and slicked back, while the other was shorter, spiked in many different areas, to give the impression of actual bed-head, and also filled with copious amounts of product. The two of them were waxing on about a poet that had grown in popularity recently, bragging how they had read him before he was mainstream. They argued over which of his poems in his collection was the best, and while I had never heard of Neal Junior, they used words like genius, genuine, honest, and believable. These were not the people who possessed secrets that would give me a reprieve. The biggest secret they held was they didn't actually read any of the stuff they bragged about reading, they had just seen a review on some trendy vlog and were regurgitating the same bile they had heard someone else, more trendy than themselves say.

To my right was a group of coworkers who were dressed in the fashion of those who spent too long at the office for one day. The men's ties were loosened, their previously crisp shirts were rumpled, and jackets had been completely abandoned. The women were all in the same fashion, shirts obviously worn throughout a day either filled with boredom and nothing to do but slump down in their ergonomic chairs while secretly checking social media sites on their phones, or stress, causing them to run frantically from meeting to meeting with little time to care about the quality of their clothing. They continually bitched about a boss or coworkers who weren't there, while pouring beers, wine, and bourbon and colas down their throats with little to no care about the people who were surrounding them. Not one of them had acknowledged my existence at the bar, which was not a new phenomenon for me, but this also lead me to believe they were unaware of my existence. I was pretty sure that soon one of the women would be pulling another to the side soon to admit something to her. It would be there my euphoria would lie. It would be there I would be able to get back to being myself. It was there my transformation would begin.

18

The great thing about having a television on at a bar is that if you are watching it, and seem to be there by yourself, everybody will leave you alone. They will assume you are completely and totally entranced by whatever is on and essentially leave you alone. This was one of the many things I had learned in my quest to be invisible. While I had decided to be more outgoing, old habits did, in fact, die hard. There was something inherently wonderful about passing through life unnoticed. It gave me freedoms nobody else would ever truly understand. While I may be considered an outcast by many, or a pariah by a few uninformed people, I knew I was living an enlightened, and heightened existence where I could create my own world, and destroy it all in the same thought. I could essentially live like a god, while others were mere mortals sneaking off to live their fantasies, while I made their lives worthy of existence. Whatever they did with their lives was nothing compared to what I created for them in my mind. If they ever had the opportunity to know what sort of grand reality they experienced within the confines of my brain they would probably realize the futility of their actual lives, causing them to wish they were no longer alive. It's probably a good thing I kept them secret. I would hate to have something such as someone's suicide hanging over my head.

I watched as whatever new, flashy, ESPN anchor got ready to announce what was possibly his very first Top Ten plays, being that I had never seen his perfectly coiffed hair, or perfectly white smile before, but he may have been there for months, and I wouldn't have known the difference. I was half paying attention to what was happening on the television in front of me, the rest of me was carefully, methodically, listening. I wanted something to come from the girls who were standing directly behind me, speaking quietly to their own ears, but loudly to anyone who hadn't been slamming vodka tonics with lime for the last few hours. I had seen this pattern hundreds, if not thousands, of times before. Soon one of them would want to confess something, anything. It was human nature to release secrets into the universe. Nobody liked to live with the burgeoning darkness, welling up inside of them, for days, weeks, months, or years, until it began to rot them from the inside, and they had to let it out, or they would be suddenly forced to deal with something subconsciously, in a much more dramatic, or dangerous way.

"Can you keep a secret?" I heard a much deeper, while still feminine, voice than I expected. I smiled. The fact was nobody would ever say no to that question. The cliffhanger question would always lead people to say yes. That would be the conversational version of having an exceptionally good television show have a season finale where it ends with a "To Be Continued" and then it never would come back. The questions floating around in the minds of the fans would never be answered, causing anger, hatred and contempt for studios, executives, and advertisers. A conversation ending the same way would essentially ruin friendships, while one attempts to imagine what the evil secret could have been. They would have had their chance to know the answers, but now, stuck in a dark world of their own imagination and hyperbolic ideas, they are left wanting for what once could have been theirs, but slipped through the wiry fingers of honesty.

"You can't let anyone know," the girl who held the secret said, as quietly as she possibly could, and even though I couldn't see her, I could tell that she had just carefully scanned the faces of bar patrons who also were sitting around after work enjoying their cocktails, and talking about the terrible jobs they had. "I slept with Chris."

My ears perked up a little. This was not that big on a secret scale, but I felt as though there was more. She was holding back, attempting to feel out how her friend felt about her statement before continuing.

"Chris Franklyn?" the friend asked, and even though there was no audible answer, I was certain the answer had been "yes" based on the amount of giggling and congratulations that were poorly being muffled behind me. "What about Jacob?"

There was the next part of the secret. The girl who slept with Chris almost undoubtedly had a boyfriend, husband, fiancé, and had cheated on him...either that or Chris did.

"I just don't have the same feelings for him anymore," she said. "I know I need to just end it with him, but I just can't, he's too crazy and could possibly hurt himself like he tried to do the last time."

There it was, my muse was cheating on her boyfriend, a young man named Jacob, with another named Chris, and she was worried about what would happen if the former would find out about the torrid affair. With that, I could work. With that, I would be able to find my way back to being a human being.

I shifted slightly in my seat in order to attempt to get a better look at who was speaking. I caught out of the corner of my eye a lovely brunette, with Eastern European, or possibly Russian features. She had beautiful hair, and it was obvious she took time every day to make it look the way it did. Her eyes were dark, and lips were pouty. Her shirt was a dark and flowy button down that clung to her breasts with all the mystery of a teenage boy feeling under a girl's shirt for the very first time. Her pants clung to her hips and buttocks accentuating what many may have considered to be her finest features, but I would have imagined she showed them off because she felt as though she didn't have what was necessary to succeed on the inside. I could see why guys such as Chris would find her attractive, but the truth of the matter was she was a cheater, and I knew I never could be with a cheater because there would never be enough trust between us to make a relationship work. This, though, was not about her and me, everything that would happen between us would only be for me, and only in my imagination, no matter how attractive I may have found her, or how much I had judged her already.

I closed my eyes, feeling the condensation of the beer trickling down the glass bottle of sub-par beer I drank. I cleared my head of all thoughts not having to do with this girl, and what she had revealed to her confidant, and me. Now was the time where I would allow myself to fade away into my own world, a world in which I wouldn't be held back by restrictions and rules. I would create this world, and in it, I would create her a story that would begin at the moment in which she and I both stood. If she was the type who believed in a multiverse I may have been able to convince her that somewhere, out in the cosmos, this life I would create actually existed, and it was there she would be able to find her true happiness.

She would leave the bar that night, a little tipsy, happy to have relieved herself of the burdensome secret that had been weighing her down for what had seemed like an eternity. It was because of the weight being lifted from her shoulders that she would take out her phone and make the phone call that she had wanted to make since lunch that day.

Her hands, nervous with anticipation, clumsily dialed the numbers, requiring her to hit the backspace button on her phone screen. With each passing ring, her heart would beat a little faster, her hope that someone would answer soon would not turn out to be futile, for by the third ring the voice she had so longed to hear could come through the receiver, "Hey, you."

"Hey there," she said. "What are you up to?"

"Not much," Chris answered. "Sitting here at home just finished making some dinner, and watching a little TV. Do you want to join me?"

He knew she was in a relationship, but he didn't care. He had been hiding his feelings for her for years now, and now that they had experienced the joy of being together he wasn't going to let her out of his grasp. The time of being passive and understanding had been left by the wayside the moment where he had carefully, nervously slid his hand softly around the back of her neck, underneath her gorgeous hair, and he gently guided her face toward his. The memory of their kiss was one he knew he would cherish for the rest of his life, and when he bragged to his friends about finally sharing something so special with this girl who they all had heard these amazing stories about, he shyly admitted this was something more than the conquests he normally bragged about. This was a girl he didn't want to stop kissing. This was the girl he attempted to kiss until the day they finally parted ways, after years, and years of a life filled with every cliche he had sworn he didn't want in his life. No, Chris wasn't giving up on her now.

"Absolutely," she said, pulling up to the stop sign near her house, and turning around to go be with him. She smiled as she drove because she also had wanted to be with him longer than she was willing to admit to her friends, family, or anyone who truly mattered in life. She knew this was the man she wanted to spend the rest of her life with, and come hell or high water; she was going to be with him. She, too, cherished the moment in which they finally kissed, telling people it was the embodiment of every school girl ideal she had about what kisses were supposed to be, and how love was supposed to feel. When she was alone, without the unwanted, or unwavering companionship of her boyfriend, she would think of that moment and be able to reach climax with just the use of her imagination, and it was better than any physical relationship she shared with any of the few men who could say they had shared a bed with her. Chris was the one, and she knew that a long time ago. Now was their moment and all signs pointed to this being a moment that would stretch out in all directions for eternity, and beyond.

She arrived at Chris's house and joined him inside, where they sat on the couch watching television, her head nestled neatly in the crook of his shoulder, his arm draped over hers. They laughed at all the same jokes and felt sorrow at all the same points, and soon it was obvious to them, along with everyone who knew them both, including Jacob, that they were destined to be together. While their trajectory was anything short of the standard, and there were bumps and roadblocks that caused unforeseen turbulence, the two of them ended up stronger after each hurdle and their souls closer than they had been previously.

She may have cried on their wedding day, but that came more from the oddly euphoric pain of childbirth than the elation she felt to be part of Chris's life forever finally, and the two of them would look down upon their child every anniversary and remember how all three of them joined as a family synchronously. The happiness and joy they would feel remembering that moment would remain resolute throughout their lives, even when struggling through the dark times, and the tears that fell at their son's funeral would not mar the connection the two of them shared but instead drove them closer together cherishing the memories they had of the boy, and the times they had all spent together.

Throughout trial and triumph, heartbreak and joy, the two of them grew together in every way. They didn't just become used to each other, they continued to learn about, and from, each other. And even though the two of them never had another child, the legacy they left in the lives and hearts of their friends and family was passed along. When Chris passed, shortly after their 65th anniversary, she was by his bedside, holding his hand, wiping his mouth, being sure to flip his pillow every 30 minutes so he would be able to enjoy the cool sensation in the final moments.

From the moment they met the two of them knew they had a special connection, and until the day she finally let go, one year to the day after Chris had moved on, they proved to the world that real love existed in this world. This was not the love people saw in movies or the love people dreamed of when they were feeling alone, this was real and in the final moments before she took her last breath she looked into the eyes of her confidant, the same one who was the first she admitted her affair with Chris too, and asked her a simple question, "Can you keep a secret?"

The confidant nodded, while lightly stroking her still perfect hair, holding back the tears she knew would soon become uncontrollable.

"I loved him with more than I knew I possessed," she said.

"I know you did, sweetie," the confidant's hand being careful not to muss her hair.

"My only regret was," she said with a slight smile. "I didn't tell him earlier."

Her eyes closed, her mouth remained the same slight smile, and her confidant knew she was no longer in the body before her. She could be felt though, somewhere in the air between the living and the dead, still looking over her confidant, keeping a caring hand on a shoulder to help ease the pain one feels when losing a dear friend, only leaving to be reunited with her love after acceptance of her passing had occurred.

That was when I opened my eyes, motioning to the bartender with the cute gap in her front two teeth that I was ready for my check, and I knew I could go home, feeling complete for the first time in longer than I cared to think about. That night I would sleep, better than I had slept in longer than I could remember, and I would be able to feel as though I was human, a feeling I had almost forgotten.

19

The next morning I awoke feeling refreshed and renewed. I didn't remember any of my dreams from the night before, but that was nothing new. I never had much recollection of what occurred in my subconscious during the night. I always felt a mixture of awe, and doubt, whenever I spoke to someone who claimed they remembered their dreams and the amount of detail in which they would tell their stories. For me sleep was a way to recharge, I didn't need to watch strange and indecipherable movies during this time, I just wanted to wake up and not feel like I had just been running through the forest being chased by a three-headed monster in which one was a dragon breathing fire, another one my father, reminding me about how I had so much potential when I was a child, and I just haven't been living up to it, and the other Hillary Clinton. I don't need to inform people of the parables that occur while I'm asleep because I don't remember them. Also, what I have found was that most people didn't care to hear about my real life, so why would they care about one my brain created due to randomly firing synapses and strange feelings any shrink would say I secretly possess for my mother. What mattered to me was the feeling of refreshment and energy to start the day anew. I could go catch a movie later if I wanted to.

I couldn't remember the last time I had woken up feeling as good as I did that morning. It had been months, maybe even longer. Most mornings I awoke feeling like I hadn't slept at all. If I didn't know any better, I would think I was living a double life. By day I was a mild-mannered, quiet, secluded individual who got his kicks by going to bars and making up stories about the people around him. By night, though, I was the life of the party, a force with which to be reckoned. I had friends of all statures, across the globe, and everyone was not only glad to know me, but they cherished my friendship. I would show up to parties and they would beg me to regale them with the old yarn of my cross-country trip to be with my girlfriend when I was only a teenager or the one where I recalled the sexual encounter I experienced with a lover I once had which involved the mishandling of hot peppers, unprotected sex, and glass of ice cold whole milk. We would all laugh and carry on into the wee hours of the morning, drinking, doing drugs, and inhaling life deep into our lungs as though that night would be our last. Every morning when I opened my eyes I should have been celebrating yet another epic night, and, more importantly, surviving it.

Unfortunately, that wasn't me. That was only someone I could dream of being if I ever dreamed. Instead, I was just a man. A man many would have considered to be inconsequential and characterless, and that would only be if the person making the statement could recall ever meeting, or having any sort of social interaction with me. I understood my lot in life, and I was no longer willing to lie back and accept it as scripture. The fact I had arisen with such vigor that morning meant things were changing, and I was going to be able to grow. I wanted to wake up with this feeling every morning. I was going to have to do that again tonight. Hell, who says I would have to wait for a night? I could go out anytime I wanted to. Everywhere across the globe there were alcoholics drinking too much in the middle of the day. Eventually, I would hear one of them confess a secret I could spin into my own brand of a perfect life.

I jumped out of my bed, that was too big for one person to be sleeping in. One day I would be able to say I shared that bed with someone other than her. I could feel myself getting closer to the person I wanted to become. I was going to have to increase the quality of the stories I created in my head. The grander and more amazing I could make the stories I played out in my imagination, the more comfortable I would be in the "real life" everyone else lived in. I wanted to be able to talk to people in this world, but until I felt as though I was one of them, or at least on the same wavelength as them, I would continue to be the broken shell of a person sitting at the corner of the bar finding contentment in my solitary life. Fortunately, I had been blessed with a gift. I could lie to myself about almost anything in the world, except that I was just a sad individual, who had more trouble making friends than a turtle does getting off of its back. If I could lie to myself about the world around me, continually making myself believe that I was more important than I, unfortunately, knew I was, I would soon be able to interact with the people who saw the world as their playground as opposed to their mausoleum.

I used to believe the shower was the best part of my day. No matter what happened the rest of the day would be less fulfilling than the moment where I washed off all of the dirtiness and sin from the entire day, and the night before. Now though, I was filled with something I wasn't used to experiencing. I had a feeling of hope welling up within me. I had hope that today was going to be better than my shower. I believed I had the opportunity to make today better than I imagined it could be. I had read a story once about two philosophers who came up with a theory called 'Two is Less Than or Equal to Four' or '$2 \leq 4$'." Essentially they were saying that everyone in the world lives their life as a two, only a few truly special and dedicated people can make their lives a four. This morning I was filled with promise that I could be one of those special people who lived their lives as a four. I had become convinced that I was one of those people who one day people would be able to talk about in song, or as an urban legend.

"He may not have done much at the beginning of his life," they would say. "But one day he began to see the error of his ways and turned his life around. He started to live a life he imagined was possible, and with that he became well-known, and well-liked by people all across the world. He truly turned his life around once he saw the error of the way he had been living. He became a person others would look up to, a mentor to children and adults alike. He was truly an inspiration."

I would become the figure people told their kids about, urging them to be more like me. I wouldn't be the shy, quiet, weird guy at the bar nobody knew or talked to. I would be the guy at the bar everybody wanted to get to know and be friends with. I felt as the water cascaded from my head, over my face, down my chest, and over my abs, a much younger and more depressed me would have lamented for not being as defined or apparent as I wanted them to be, and I felt as though I was being born anew. This must be what all the people who were always coming to my door and attempting to get me to accept Jesus as my savior were always clamoring on about. They always talked about this feeling of being alive, as though everything you had done in your past didn't matter anymore. Every mistake, every wrong decision, every questionable act I had ever committed would be washed away they promised. At this moment I knew what they were referring to, as I was no longer worried about what was going to happen with my days because I knew everything was going to be ok.

I jumped out of the shower and toweled off. I was ready for this day to begin. I was ready for more than just this day to begin; I was ready for this life to begin. The next step in my rehabilitation into a normal and functioning person was to find a bar filled with a good amount of people that would be unfazed by a newcomer in their midsts. There I would be able to create another dimension to my world. With each passing story my world would continue to grow stronger, and in those walls I would realize my full potential as a person who was good enough to be around the people who walked around the real world, not realizing anything that was going on around them. I would finally be accepted, and no longer would I be alone.

20

In the darkest dredges of the city, in the areas of town most people would be wary of venturing to, with the exceptions the USPS and other delivery men, would be the place where I found the bar with people who had no issue with a newcomer among them. They were more worried about how long it would be until the owners of the property they were illegally squatting in found out about them, than a new face quietly sipping on a beer, eyes plastered to the television that barely could support cable, much less have anything shown on it in High Definition. This was the type of establishment where secrets festered until the stench became so unbearable the bar shut down rather than let the secrets out of their cages. In a place like this, I would have to exercise patience while waiting for my indulgence to be fulfilled, but it was with patience that great rewards were given. My reward was to become one step closer to greatness, while slowly understanding more about the human condition so many people seemed to suffer from.

I walked in and could smell the smoke that hung in the air from years of smokers meandering about the bar area, cigarette hanging from their lips, smoke wafting upwards as their eyes stared down at the ground searching for some sort of solace in their lives. Even though the city had placed a ban on cigarettes in bars, they didn't care. This was not the type of establishment the city council was worried about. They were concerned with chain restaurants, and popular college hangouts. They were attempting to enforce their government mandated protection on people who were contributing members of society. Not a single member of the council was worried about a bar where every person ordering drinks had already died in their own eyes. While I knew there was no real secret that would surprise me in this bar, there would definitely be a story or two I would be able to turn into my own mental release.

The bartender spotted me as soon as I entered the bar. Her eyes locking on me, a new customer, one with a name she didn't know and followed me across the bar to where I sat down. Her eyes were steely blue, and her hair was died a color blonde that was too blonde for anyone to believe it was natural. Faded tattoos covered her body, each a testament to a different bad decision she had made in her life. She would probably tell a customer that she still liked and cherished each one, but when she was at home, kept company by her malnourished cats, she would look at herself in the mirror and wonder what she may look like now without all of the faded blues, greens and reds scattered across her body.

Slowly she walked over to me, staring at me the entire way, as though I may pull out a badge at any second and shut down the bar she had called home for what I could only assume was an embarrassing amount of time. Stopping at the register, she pulled a cigarette out of a pack under the bar and lit it, taking an elongated drag from the filtered end, fearing this one, just like so many others before it, may be her last. She took the last few steps approaching me, one hand braced on her hip, and with every ounce of contempt she had inside of her body she looked at me in my eyes and asked,

"What can I get ya?"

I smiled and told her I would like a Bud Light. She sighed, as though it is the last thing in the world she wanted to serve, and walked back down to the other side of the bar, muttering under her breath the entire way. She pulled a bottle out of a broken down looking refrigerator and made her way back across the bar to hand me my beer.

"Two twenty-five," she said, cigarette never moving from her lips.

I reached into my pocket and pulled out a five spot, which I then handed to her. She grabbed it from my hands and walked over to the register, still muttering to herself with each step. She was evidently not pleased with the presence of a stranger in their midsts and had little to no qualms with displaying her distrust and hatred for me. The sound of the register opening dinged throughout the bar, and I watched as she made my change. Slowly she walked back, cigarette never wavering from the spot in her mouth, and she slapped the money down on the area in front of me. I glanced down at the crumpled up money and dingy quarters sitting at the base of my bottle, and I chuckled to myself as I noticed she had only given me back $2.50.

I decided not to say anything about the shortage of money and just concentrate on what I was there to do. The loss of a quarter was worth the experience I was after. I wanted to feel how I felt last night, and how I felt this morning, and the way to do that was to listen to the stories the old salts were spinning, and not quibble over essentially the cost of a stale gumball. Instead, I picked up my beer and took a long, slow, sip out of the head of the bottle. Glancing up at the television I tried squinting to make out the images from ESPN flashing somewhere from behind the static and snow on the face of a television that was by this point old enough to drink if it had been a person. The entire bar was the building equivalent of a time capsule. It was as though somebody put the entire thing together 40 years prior and nothing had been updated, with the exception of liquor, since. The tap handles were rusty and appeared as though they haven't been cleaned since their installation. A thin layer of dust and smoke clung to every inch of the bar. Even the floors looked like they had only been half-assed swept since the day the doors opened.

I wrapped my fingers around my beer and quickly deduced that the refrigerator they were using was working improperly as well, due to the lukewarm state of the bottle. I brought it to my lips and took a long sip anyway. I figured complaining about it would do nothing more than get me booted from the bar, and I wouldn't achieve my end goal of creating a new section of my world and feel like I was human again. I choked down the cheap tasting beer and attempted to focus all of my energy on the snowed out television.

The other bar patrons spoke softly to each other. There was no need for them to shout in this crowd, nobody else was fighting for the attention of whomever they were talking to. I was straining to pick up any sort of conversation, and even that was resulting in only a mixed sample of words and phrased that meant little to nothing without knowing the full context of the conversation. Most of them seemed to just be slurring their words together into one elongated word they were attempting to pass off as a complete sentence. The only phrases I was ever able to make out were "When I was in Viet Nam," and "That bitch took everything." I realized I had become trapped in a cliché with no way to achieve my goal except to engage those around me in conversation. I was going to have to get them to talk to me about their problems, and from there I would be able to blossom slightly more.

I cautiously looked around the bar, not wanting to engage any of the regulars in a mistaken look of aggression. I just wanted to carefully, and in a non-threatening manner grab someone's attention, and entice them into a conversation with a friendly, and apathetic nod of the head. The only question left was as to whom I would extend my friendly gesture. Glancing around I could see that most of the others were already engaged in talks with another individual who was only half listening to whatever bullshit was being spewed by the drunk talking about their glory days, and how everything went wrong due to one tragedy or another.

Finally, my eyes quickly locked with those of an older gentleman at the end of the bar and, as to not appear rude, I gave him the nonchalant head nod and continued to look around the bar, ending up back on the television I was attempting to watch. Soon after, I saw out of the corner of my eye as the gentleman picked up his beer, stood up, and started walking in my direction. His tall, slender, frame stumbled across the dirty concrete floor, almost falling a time or two before arriving at the seat next to me. He pulled out the broken down stool and sat down.

"HeyThere," he said, his words blending together into one. "I'mJimmy."

Jimmy's breath wreaked of beer and cigarettes. Veins were painted across the now yellowed canvas that used to be the whites of his eyes. His mustache was a brilliant white and was stained with liquor, much like the department store Santa Claus I had seen in the malls around Christmas. He wore a trucker hat with the picture of a U.S. Naval ship on it. His clothes hung off of him as though he had bought them when he was a much heavier individual and had simultaneously lost weight and any money he could have used to purchase new ones. His teeth were stained brown and yellow from, what I could only assume was, years of smoking the heavily tarred cigarettes.

He reached his hand out to greet me. I looked down at the thin hand, noticing that it appeared as though the skin had been stretched over it, like plastic wrap over Tupperware, and covered with dark spots. I reached out and grabbed it, shaking firmly to assert my manliness. I could tell Jimmy didn't want to talk to anyone who had never worked with his hands. He only wanted to talk to manly men. Men who had worked on their cars themselves. Men who knew how to gut a fish they had actually caught. Men who put their self-worth into their woodwork.

"LetMeTellYouSomething," Jimmy said, his words welded together in an ever-changing tonal buzz. "WhenIWasInVietnamIWatchedAsMyFuckingFriendFucking DiedRightInFront OfMe."

I was taken aback at the beginning of this conversation. Jimmy hadn't wasted any time with any sort of pleasantries, he jumped right into the deep end of the pool with both feet first, not even checking to see if there was water. If there was anyone in the bar who was going to be able to tell me a secret I would be able to get off to, this would be the man. I repositioned myself away from the television and turned toward Jimmy, showing him that he had 100% of my attention.

This tactic seemed to do the trick because as soon as I turned toward him, he seemed to get even more engaged with me. His face brightened up, probably at the idea of anyone willing to listen to him. He turned slightly more in my direction and took a quick, yet full drink from his beer.

"WeWereOnlyKids,Man," he said. "WeShouldn'tHaveEvenBeenOverThere. HeDefinitely Shouldn'tHaveDiedOverThere. IWatchedHimGetHisHeadBlownOff. ItStillHurtsToThink AboutToday."

Jimmy's yellowed eyes began to water. I could only imagine the amount of pain he was living with after experiencing something of that nature. Even though I never had the opportunity to be close enough to anyone to call them my best friend, I would think I would hold onto the pain for the rest of my life as well. I could see that Jimmy needed someone to talk to, an ear to listen to his story and someone who could sympathize with what he had been living with for so long.

"WhenWeLeftHomeToGoThere," he said, a tear falling from his eye. "WeWeren'tSureIfWe WouldEvenComeHome. IWasLucky,HeWasNot."

I began to feel for Jimmy. I could see how he had started drinking the amount he had. Leaving home at a young age, going halfway across the globe to fight in a war he may not have believed in, but he had no choice because an arbitrary number was called. He was trained to kill, and then he was sent out and expected to just that. His friends may have looked down upon him for not running, and the fact he may have killed people while deployed may have made them question his morals, even though he was just doing what he had been told. After coming home he thought he was going to get a hero's welcome, but instead, he was shunned, and his government essentially cast him to the side in a sea of other soldiers who never got what they were promised, nor did they give them a shred of the medical help they had promised them.

"IRememberSittingAtMyMom'sHouseRightBeforeILeft," he said. "ThatSong "HookedOnAFeeling"
byBlueSwedeWasPlaying. ItWasAlwaysPlaying.
ItWasSuchABigHit. WeWereOnThePorchSingingThatSong..."

Jimmy started to laugh. A strange maniacal laugh grew as he started repeating the phrase "Ooga Chaga, Ooga Ooga Chaga, Ooga Chaga, Ooga Ooga Chaga" over and over again. With each repetition, his laugh grew louder, more maniacal, and gave me time to think. I knew the Viet Nam War ended by the end of 1973. I also knew that song came out in 1974.

Jimmy was lying to me, to what degree I couldn't be sure, but I knew he was lying. In his own unintentional way, he was telling me his secret. He never went to Viet Nam, and he never watched his friend die, over there at least.

A smile crossed my face as I turned away from Jimmy. I didn't need to hear anything else from him. He was completely full of shit, and the life I was about to create for him in my head had a decently good chance to more historically accurate than the story he had been telling anybody who was willing to listen. I wrapped my fingers around the now exceptionally warm beer bottle and closed my eyes. I heard Jimmy still talking to me, but nothing else mattered. He had given me what I wanted from him. Anything else he would say would just aid in ruining the story I was going to work up about him. Anybody who was willing to lie about his military service, and how and where he lost a friend didn't deserve any sort of redemption. I just allowed myself to fade away as his voice dissipated more and more until I didn't hear it all anymore. I had escaped to my happy place.

I saw the world in 1973 when all of the soldiers had returned home from the war. Jimmy was out of high school, but his number had never gotten called. Even though there were stories from all over about how the soldiers weren't getting the fanfare they thought they would receive, Jimmy saw his friends who graduated with him, or the year before coming home and being treated like local idols. They were getting the jobs he never could, and getting the girls who never would give him the time of day. He wished he could receive just a fraction of the attention they were being given. He thought he had been dealt the lucky hand by not going over there, but now he wished he had been. Then he would get the recognition from his townspeople he felt he deserved.

His addiction started out simply enough. Just like the

others who were back from battle, he went out to bars and told people about his experiences in the war, spouting off from memory the stories he had heard other people say. The only problem was he still lived in the same city he had been his entire life. Soon he was being threatened by those who had actually fought in the war, and he was shunned at all the bars, and worse, by all the women he wanted to be with. Jimmy was going to have to leave his hometown if his plan was going to work.

He decided to move away from the town he grew up in and go out into the world in order to receive any sort of a hero's welcome. After taking a trip to the local Army/Navy store to load up on government issued BDUs he packed up all of his stuff and moved to the big city. He was able to find a job working for a construction company whose owner was hiring GIs, and after Jimmy told his potential boss the story of his time over in the jungle, and his personal battles with Charlie, he was hired. Jimmy took this time in order to hone his stories, making sure each detail was perfectly planned. He didn't want to say too much about what it was like to kill someone since he had never done it. Instead, he said he didn't want to talk about it, opting to act as though the pain of the issue was too severe. Anytime people started asking too many questions, looking for specifics, such as platoon numbers and locations of raids, he removed himself from the conversation, saying he was going to the bar to get another drink. A drink he would never return from getting.

He was living high through the 70's and into the early 80's, but as the decade turned five people cared less and less about the war as their attention was focused on newer and more topical issues. In order to keep people interested in his stories, Jimmy had to spice up his stories, adding parts to them the morbid nature of most people would want to hear about. It was then that Jimmy invented his best friend who died during a raid in North Vietnam during the Christmas bombings. Nobody needed to know he was still living in his Podunk town, washing car windshields at the local gas station for minimum wage during that time.

The more he told his stories, the more even he believed them. He got drinks bought for him, and people thanked him for his service to the country every time he went out. Some nights he was lucky enough to not have to pay for a drink. All he had to do was tell his stories, and people wanted him to be around. He couldn't remember a time in his life when he had been as happy as he was while he was out there telling his fictional stories. To justify his actions in his head he convinced himself he was an actor, just playing a part, but it was a part in which he would never be able to break character.

When the U.S. went to war in the Middle East people stopped caring about anyone who fought in Vietnam, now they only cared about the people who had fought in the desert. He and his veteran brothers had been forgotten. He started going out to bars, and whenever he told people he had fought in Vietnam, they didn't seem to care anymore. They were only interested in the latest war. How quickly they had forgotten all the people, who had lost their lives in the last war. Whenever he would talk to someone who didn't seem to care about Vietnam, he would get angry. His gravy train had pulled out of the station, and he had been left behind.

Unwavering in his behavior, and unwilling to change his story he continued to tell them at bars in hopes he would soon get a free beer from the bartender, or a patron who would listen to him. As he grew older, the amount of people who were willing to listen grew fewer and fewer, until he was paying for all of his drinks, and eventually buying them for people just so he would have people listen to him tell his stories.

After the turn of the century, and the country growing weary of constantly being involved in wars, he began fighting with people he assumed didn't care about veterans, or at least those who he assumed didn't care about him, which was slowly becoming the majority of people. People didn't even seem to want Jimmy to purchase them drinks anymore. He tried to get people to like him, but they didn't want to talk to him anymore. Even his coworkers at the construction company would just leave him after work. Eventually, he quit his job and started living on social security, and government welfare programs. He started spending all day in bars, sitting there, drinking bad beer, and taking shots of cheap whiskey, hoping that somebody would want to hear any of the stories he had been practicing telling for over 30 years now. Most days he just sat there by himself, until he got so drunk he would wander over to a group of younger people hanging out, talking, and just begin to spout off his stories. When they would undoubtedly make fun of him, or leave him there by himself, Jimmy would lose his temper and tell them that they needed to show him respect, because he fought in Vietnam, and Vietnam was the last real war America had been in. This would always alienate him further, as almost everyone in the younger generation had a brother, sister, neighbor, or friend who had fought in Iraq, Afghanistan, Yemen, Pakistan, or Libya.

"IDon'tGiveAFuckAboutThoseWars," he would say, his words blending together like a chainsaw buzzing. "TheyAren'tRealWars! VietnamWasTheLastRealWar!"

Usually this would end with the recipients of his comments walking away from Jimmy and making him the butt of their jokes, but on occasion he would say this to an Iraq War Vet, or to a soldier who served in Afghanistan, and Jimmy, with his lack of military training and inebriated demeanor, would end up broken and beat up in the streets. This happened so often in fact, the cops never asked why he was lying in the street when they saw him there. They would just pick him up, throw him in the back of their car, and drop him off at home before he got hurt by someone else that night.

Jimmy never could understand it had been 30 years of him talking about the war, a war he had never even fought in, and he never changed. He watched his entire life as others got recognition and praise for something he was too afraid to do, but was willing to take all of the credit for. He chalked up his problems to a country who never cared about the veterans, which was a falsity. His problems stemmed from Jimmy hating himself, and never accepting his life the way that it was. The amount of torture he put his insides through was much worse than the alcohol and cigarettes could do to him.

When Jimmy got sick, nobody seemed to notice, nor did anyone seem to care when he stopped coming around to the bars as often. As he showed up less and less, the bartenders that knew him by name started working elsewhere, and a new crew came aboard. A crew that didn't know Jimmy, his story, or want to put up with his shenanigans. Soon he was 86'd from every bar he was once considered a regular. He didn't even have anybody to call when he fell that day and had to lie there, waiting for anyone to come by to help him.

While he was lying there on the floor, staring at the ceiling, hoping the mailman would come by, or perhaps the neighbor who always wanted to borrow a tool from him, Jimmy realized he had squandered his life in every way possible. Instead of actually going out there and doing something with his life, he lied and told people he had accomplished something. It was upon realizing this that Jimmy cried real tears, not the fake ones he put on when telling about watching his best friend die in combat or remembering the face of child he shot in Hanoi, real tears that made him remember what it was to be a kid who wanted to be wanted by people in their lives. Now, he didn't want people to want him in their lives as much as he wanted anyone to be in his life. He wondered how many relationships he had ruined while telling falsities and fictitious stories about his life. Maybe if he was honest with anyone, just once, he would have someone there with him now, in his darkest moment.

The funeral director wasn't surprised when nobody showed up to his service. He had seen Jimmy around town and knew he had no friends, or family in the area who would be showing up. He was glad nobody was showing up though, it meant he got to go home early if nobody came.

I looked over at Jimmy, who was still talking to me, even though I hadn't been listening to him for quite some time now, and smiled. I finished my beer and put the empty bottle down on the bar in front of me. I stood up, watching Jimmy's face turn to one of shock as I started to walk away, never once saying a word.

"HeyManWhereAreYouGoing?" he yelled after me. "Don'tYouKnowIWasInVietnam?"

I shook my head and walked out into the daylight, shielding my eyes from the sun, glad to be out of the bar and away from Jimmy. Once again I felt human, and I hoped this feeling would last forever, but I knew that soon I would have to be back at a bar listening in on another conversation, just so I could find this sort of completeness again.

21

This is what my life became. I found myself at bars constantly, listening, waiting, wanting, hoping for anyone to admit to something around me so I could dive into my own world and create their story. This was worse than it was before. If I hadn't done this before she came into my life, nothing would change about my demeanor. Now, though, I would become agitated at the mere thought of not being able to visit my world. I found myself developing a mild shake, or have trouble sleeping at night where I would lie in bed, breaking out into strange sweats while I thought about what I may have heard if I had gone out to the bars. When I wasn't sleeping I was dreaming of a world that didn't exist, a world I created in my head, a world where I had not yet made a cameo. All of my stories involved other people, and not once did I show up in the storyline, even though in all of their real lives I had at the very least a background part. I found myself growing more depressed, and feeling more alone, but I needed to go out and be around people. I needed to be able to escape into my world, or else I would find myself collapsing in on myself, like a star that had burned out.

Day after day, night after night, I found myself at bars quietly listening. Milking my beer for as long as possible, until the hops and barley had begun to sour, the temperature had passed tepid, and the flavor stung as it dragged across my tastebuds. The television spewed information at me, but none of it ever truly mattered, not for what I was there to accomplish. I was there to find oneness with myself, and slowly I could feel I was getting closer to being the person I wanted to be. I had become the person I was before she came into my life, and now I was working on becoming the person I wished I always had the testicular fortitude to be.

The problem was I had found more enjoyment than I ever thought possible spending time in the world I was building inside my head. The time I spent there was more rewarding than any time I spent in the so-called real world. Every time I went out to the bars I had the expressed intention of having a rewarding interaction with a person that wasn't just another drunken exchange of little consequence. This dream always fell short, as everybody seemed to want to be engaged with somebody other than myself. I was finding myself with more free time than was good for me, and soon I was watching over my world. My safety blanket. My social lubricant. My escape from a reality that never truly seemed to accept me as the person I was. It was a place I felt truly free to be myself. When I would get through exploring the latest addition I would have lost all desire to communicate with anyone not on my etherial plane. I would look around the bar at all the people experiencing earth on the singular option they see, feel bad for each one of them, shake my head as I felt sorrow for each of the drunken sheep, finish my beer and then head home feeling satisfied, but lonely at the same time.

I would find myself back at my house, waiting for tired to set in so I could fall asleep, just for the opportunity to do it all again the next day. Every morning I was greeted with another opportunity to have a real-world meaningful interaction with a person, something that wouldn't make me want to retreat into my own head, and help me forget about her for good. Unfortunately, nobody in the real world seemed interested in any sort of interaction with me in which I was not paying them for their time. Slowly I was figuring out the world was filled with legal prostitutes, who were drowning their own sorrows in their daily lives of performing government approved services for money, which people who were even sadder were willing to pay.

22

More often than not I found myself at the same bar I met her at what seemed like a lifetime ago at this point. I was confidant I wasn't going to be bumping into her any time soon. She wouldn't have wanted to risk her sobriety by showing her face at a bar again, especially the last bar she went to before attending rehab. My attendance at the bar had been so regular over the past few weeks that while the blonde bartender with the cute gap in her teeth still didn't know my name, we had gotten to the point where she was handing my beer without my having to ask for it by name. While I considered this a slight personal victory, I also saw the danger that could be ahead. People seemed to gravitate to that which is familiar to them. They have their regular bars, regular drinks, regular seats at church, regular orders at restaurants, paths to work and back home every day. Falling into a pattern locks people in a lifestyle of mediocrity and mundanity. This leads to drinking more of the regular drinks, and eventually drinking too much of them. Eventually, one finds them self in such a rut that they only have the aid of what's in their drink to make them feel as though their life is new and meaningful. Then, much like she did, they find themselves with a problem they don't know how to solve, having to choose a rehabilitation of some sort, or trading it for another addiction.

Even with the impending issue of crippling alcoholism fresh on my mind as I thought about the dangers of the inevitable conclusion of falling into a predictable pattern, I was still primarily focused on the task at hand. I needed to have a meaningful interaction with someone. I recalled the less than meaningful interactions I had experienced throughout my existence and at this point was ready to settle for any of them as well. I didn't need them to know my name, or for me to know theirs for that matter. I just needed to feel as though I had engaged somebody, even if only for a simple second they would forget within a matter of hours, if not minutes. Never to be one who blamed his upbringing, or the lack of any sort of life as a child, I found myself wondering how I had failed as an adult and was causing my complete inability to engage a person who wasn't in my head.

Sipping my beer, staring up at the television, I checked out the other bar patrons through my periphery in hopes of finding anyone with whom I wasn't intimidated to speak. I cursed my inhibitions as I peered across the wooden slats which created the three-foot buffer between the drunks and the object of everyone there's affection. Once again, the bar was filled with happy hour attenders and a few competing restaurant's employees attempting to get a slight buzz before heading into their soul-sucking jobs in customer service. Everyone had already broken off into their predetermined cliques, and left sitting alone, waiting to be picked, was I. Already having trouble speaking with a solitary person injecting myself into the middle of a group dynamic was something I knew I was not yet ready to attempt. Each passing opening of the door to the outside bar area I looked with the grand hope that maybe there would be another solo person with whom I could strike up a simple conversation.

Something about the weather perhaps, because here, now, in my most desperate I was not unwilling to rely upon clichés. With each door opening came a door shutting with no reprieve for my desires, and soon I would have to realize that today was just another day where I was solidly cementing my fate as the lonely, creepy, guy at the bar who drank Bud Light and watched SportsCenter until it was time to move along.

Thankfully though, there was always time to begin listening, and with listening came a deeper understanding of people. Their dirty laundry was waiting to be hung out to dry, and their deepest desire was to feel free of their own self-loathing. This is why when people were lucky enough to find themselves immersed in the loving bosom of an accepting and caring group of friends they were wary of indulging strangers who may have seemed as though they, too, were just looking for a friend with which to talk. This was why making friends the older you got seemed to be much more difficult. Allowing ones own guards to be let down, while also penetrating the barriers put up by others, was a difficult task that slowly I was learning had become impossible without the aid of copious amounts of social lubricant, or cocaine. It was with this realization I had seen into my future of a man who was going to not only die alone, but probably with the aid of his own hands.

The darkness of my own thoughts began to weigh me down, and I concluded that I would not be reaching any social milestones this evening. Instead I would be spending yet another night in my head, void of any true redemption, but instead living in a world within the infinite bounds of my imagination. While the thought of diving off into my own world excited me still, I wanted to know what it was like to be authentic, not just the figment of a real person. It was within the dirty laundry of others where I felt real. As though I had some sort of control over a world, even if it was only a world I created. Sitting, observing, waiting for the right time to begin truly listening to what people may be saying to each other, I relaxed into my usual slouched position, hand gently cradling my beer bottle, eyes fixed upon the television even though nothing on the screen was registering in my brain.

I had grown so accustomed to the position in which I was now perched that for a brief moment, before I remembered I was hardly a real individual, I felt natural and authentic for a brief moment of glorious comfort. In the few short moments of feeling alive, I could see the world as a place where people cared for each other, not just for their own self-serving reasons but because it was what the other person needed. I saw a world where a man gives a homeless man a dollar. Not because he was filled with guilt because his life turned out better than the unfortunate person's life, nor because he was attempting to impress another person with a show of an altruistic act of charity, or even because the government, a division of law enforcement, or strong-arming non-profit told him he must give the dollar. And it especially was not because giving the dollar would make him feel good on the inside. He gave the dollar to the homeless man because deep down he didn't want to, and giving the dollar actually hurt a little and he knew that is where true charity lies.

Then I remembered I was there for a mission. Since my primary mission would not be able to be completed that evening, I was going to have to fall back onto my stand-by mission. I closed my eyes, omitting my visual sense and increasing my already rather tuned sense of hearing. With enough concentration and patience, I would begin to hear the different conversations going on around the bar without having to leave my seat. This was a skill I had utilized time and time again while creating a new section of the only world in which I was ever able to survive.

"You can normally go up to six, maybe six and a half

watts," I heard someone say, referring to a new e-cig mod he brought into the bar.

"Hey, Sean, you ready?" a girl yelled out, asking, presumably, Sean if he was ready to leave.

"You take too long," I heard a random male's voice say.

"Did you ever get the burger there?"

"Have you seen Roland?"

"I'll be back."

"Can I get another beer, and a froggy?"

"Want to go out by the fire to smoke?"

"Can I get some of that juice you're vaping?"

Random sayings, random people, just waiting for any sort of hint of a conversation that may conclude with my version of a climax tonight. People are going through their lives as though nobody else in the world existed, not worried about any other soul other than theirs. Their conversations were testaments of self-righteous indignation. Everything was filled with "I" or "me" statements, only using "You" when in need of something, or taking a person down a peg or two from the self-ordained pedestal on which many of them found themselves perched.

"You need to think about what you're saying."

"I don't want to deal with the idiots at work tonight."

"Can I borrow $20 bucks from you?"

Senseless. Meaningless. Unnecessary words creating boring and clichéd conversations that could be heard across the globe in a thousand languages, in a thousand bars. It was a result of the same programming that I too fell, victim. We are told we are special and don't let anyone tell you any differently. The dark secret is that we aren't all special. Instead, only a handful of people throughout history could actually lay claim to that title. For the rest of us, we are forgettable, and already have been by over eighty percent of the people we have met over the course of our lives.

"You hook up with her?"

"Oh, what was that girl's name?"

"You are such a slut."

"Coming from the man-whore."

Insults and barbs are thrown across the air as friends and acquaintances said anything they could in order to make themselves feel better about their own poor choices in life. Each word doing nothing more than driving a thicker wedge deeper into already cracked and broken relationships built on the weak foundation of alcohol and cigarettes.

Through the crap and the monotony of discussions falling miles short of originality, there seemed to be a lacking sense of educated debate about anything. This was why people had become obsessed with knowing the secrets of friends and strangers, and this is why people loved to have them. It allowed them a break from the everyday bullshit they waded through attempting to make a memorable night out of humdrum dreariness. This was why I was always able to get what I needed out of a night, by escaping to a world that wasn't so predictable.

"Hey, come here," I heard a female voice say. My ears perked up at the obvious attempt to separate one from the proverbial herd, in order to get him alone. Often I had heard men do this in order to get women away from other women I had heard referred to as mother hens. It was on a rare occasion I heard a woman do this with a man, unless it was an ex-boyfriend situation, and his friends were against their reuniting. "I want to talk to you."

A smile crossed my face as I knew how this story was about to unfold. These two were probably among the group of restaurant workers, and they had been battling with a will-they-won't-they situation for a while now. She had been waiting for him to make the first move, afraid of hurting the friendship she had built up in her mind. The tension had probably grown too much for her, and now she was just hoping he wasn't sleeping with someone else. Soon would come the wonderful words I longed to hear day after day, and even though I knew how every portion of this story ended. In real life she would have her heart broken, in my world though, she would have finally confronted and found her life long love.

The grip on my bottle tightened ever so slightly. I was able to tune out every other conversation occurring in the bar that evening. It was as though in the infinite void of darkness that everyone merely moved through I was able to make it only the three of us in the bar at that moment. They had no idea I was listening in on their conversation, just like everyone else who had come before them, and presumably, everyone who would come after them. It was where so many liked to hide unsuccessfully, but where I had found a home, albeit, a home I didn't want, but instead a home I was shackled to, like the millions of people who bought a house before the housing crash and were stuck where they were living for the unforeseeable future. One day I would move away from the prison where I had locked myself, but it would require something greater than failed government bailouts, and market corrections. The truth was, the relocation of my personality, much like most relocations that occurred was completely and utterly dependent upon myself.

The conversation they had begun was filled with basic fillers, nothing of any real substance, just dancing around the subject at hand in hopes the other one would find the courage to bring it up to the other. "How are you?" and "Can you believe what so and so did at work the other day?" type of questions, while not facing the real reason they decided to peel away from the already perfectly fitted group. Perhaps they were concerned with what their friends may think, while in the grand scheme of honesty, they probably already knew. Also, when dealing with restaurant workers, they are one of the closest-knit groups ever put together. Theirs is a true family dynamic, but as people leave due to life taking them on to better things, or moving to a new city, or getting fired for one too many customer complaints they are typically quickly forgotten, and the ones who remain close will struggle to remember the names of even those they considered brothers. If these two could realize these facts they would be able to cut past all of the bullshit and canned conversations they were currently having and get to the real meat of the issue staring them both in the face...sex.

The obviousness of their actions was only masked by the glowing aura of a perceived friendship that had blossomed between the two of them. She may have had a boyfriend when they met, and now after he wanted to look like the good guy and act as solely her friend. Now, afraid of ruining another falsified friendship by expressing his true intentions he was deciding to live in the background, hoping she would make the first move before she found somebody else. While the girl of his affection obviously longed for him to grab hold of her with both arms and kiss her like they were in a Frank Capra movie, even if she had absolutely zero knowledge of who Frank Capra was.

Flirtation and attraction, parry and thrust, search and destroy. The artistic nature of picking someone up in a bar was a dance that few had truly mastered, and this young gentleman was not one of those people. I had observed while people had flirted their way into the girls bathroom of a bar in less time than it had taken him even to broach the subject of what they were thinking about doing after work that night. I could hear him subliminally screaming out for another shot of liquid courage, so he could just get the guts to blurt out how he felt about her.

Both of them were playing a boring game of relationship

chicken, and while they were betting on the other person to make the first move, the rest of the world paying attention was betting against them both. They were failing at the one specific human instinct that was possessed by all mankind. I shook my head and scoffed an ironic scoff as he had already accomplished more in ten minutes than I had been able to in a lifetime. This was part of the reason I lived vicariously through the people I overheard at bars. Their lives would be the fuel that stoked the fire that was my will to continue on in a world where I had very little chance of creating a meaningful connection with anyone ever again.

I could feel my need for them to expose themselves to each other growing with each passing second. My heart began to palpitate faster. A slight glint of sweat began to bead across my forehead. My hands began to tremor with a slight shake that, while maybe nobody noticed, seemed to be more dramatic than a California earthquake. I squeezed my hands into fists as I attempted to quell the shaking. I clinched my teeth, and closed my eyes as I focused every ounce of my being on listening, just wanting to hear the words I needed to hear. I knew I was beginning to crave this more than I had ever thought possible, or had ever craved anything before. I could feel tears welling up within my eyes as I worked ever so hard to not look like the crazy freak at the bar, but with each passing second as the boy and the girl wearing their not quite pristine restaurant uniforms, and saturated with Tennessee whiskey and vodka droned on about absolutely nothing, and everything at the exact same time. How could they be talking about something so mundane, and so inconsequential while I could tell they were living with pain in their hearts? I wanted to turn around, look at them in their evil eyes, and scream at them for holding me back, for not giving me what I needed at that moment. They were hindering my progress in becoming a new and wonderful person. I wanted to be free from these shackles. I wanted to feel what people who knew how to feel felt. I wanted to know what it was like to take air, not in the way that so many people meandered through the day, just breathing in and out, but I wanted to be able to tell people what air actually tasted like, and it was all supposed, to begin with these two, what seemed to be, obviously soon-to-be workplace lovers. They were the only escape I had from the incarceration with which I had burdened myself. I picked up my beer, finishing the entire thing in a single gulp, and slamming the bottle on the bar as though I was attempting to show the world that I was all that is man, and look at what I did with my beer.

The cute bartender looked at me. I pointed to my bottle, and I nodded, notifying her I was ready for another one. I lowered my head into my hands and wished I could be anyone else in the world. In all of my self-pity and sorrow I sat there wishing I could change my life the way nobody else had ever truly been able to, when I finally heard the words I had been waiting for the entire time I had been sitting at the bar, "Can you keep a secret?"

My head perked up; my whole body was reinvigorated by life. I felt like a junky who had finally gotten a hit of heroin, an alcoholic who had just gotten a sip of whiskey, or what she probably felt like whenever she had met someone she would be able to take home with her, much as how she did for me. The tremor in my hands subsided, the bead of sweat seemed to magically dissipate instantly, the urge to scream and yell at people disseminated into the normal contempt for everything I had grown accustomed to over the course of the 33, almost 34, years I had been in existence. I could breath, and it felt good, the same way it felt when she and I spent that night together. The way it felt when she and I hung out, just talking, while waiting through long nights for the sun to come up to end the darkness she was living with. Instantly, I was whole again.

I wrapped my fingers around the ice cold bottle of Bud Light the cute bartender had placed in front of me, and waited for the next portion of the conversation. It wouldn't matter what the secret was; I was going to take it and run with it, farther than I had ever allowed my mind to go before, and farther than I would ever allow my mind to go again. I was going to take it to an area where even I would question the boundaries of fiction and reality. An area that would be occupied by nobody other than myself and my thoughts. A place in the subconscious meek minded people would never be able to return from if they had ever allowed themselves to get that deep. I wanted to be able to detach myself from my psyche and hover above all of my thoughts, dreams, and fantasies, and watch them play out like a movie on a screen where I was the ultimate director, and I controlled everything and everyone. I was the Messiah. I was omnipotent. I was the alpha, the omega, and everything in between. It all started now.

I looked up at the television, the flashing lights and quintessential programming seemed to go by in a pixellated mess as I waited for the continuation of the conversation. Everybody lied when asked that question. The answer was always "yes" and this time would be no different. I just had to wait for the recipient of the query to answer the answer that everybody gave.

"Can you keep a secret?" I heard the voice asked again. Still, no answer had come, and the person wanting to unburden themselves of their guilt seemed to be getting impatient by the lack of the response, as was I.

"Can you keep a secret?" I heard once again, this time it was attached to tap on my shoulder, and I turned to see who was repeating the question I had wanted to hear for what seemed like an eternity.

I inhaled deeply, afraid it may be the last breath I would ever take. Once again I was certain I had begun to tremble so noticeably that the group of people next to me would soon begin complaining there drinks were splashing over the sides of their respective sized glasses. Unsure of what to say, or what to do, I continued drinking from my beer, holding onto it like a child holding on to his or her security blanket when in a crowd full of strangers. There was something frightening, and also consoling, brewing from somewhere deep inside of me as I realized I was staring directly into her crystal blue eyes.

23

"Well," she said. "Can you?"

I didn't know what to say. I felt myself lost as I looked into the eyes I had stared into the night after night as I wished that they would be the portals to the secret to hearing the words I had wanted to hear since the day she and I met. Her hair slightly tussled, and smile just as crooked and sexy as it ever had been. I wanted to yell at her and tell her just to leave me alone. I wanted to kiss her deeply, the way a man kisses the clitoris of the woman he loves, and only for the woman he loves. Not the half-assed way he does on a random bar skank he just picked up while drunk and looking for a night of stress relief. The secret there being she is doing the same thing, and while he considers her a bar skank, she considers him a threat to her name, her credibility, whatever purity she has left, as well as her life. His sexist stereotyping would continue to be a problem throughout the rest of his life, while her guarded nature, while occasionally letting the walls down, would be the only things that protected her from creeps worse than a sexist asshole.

I nodded, but without any true belief in the action, I had just made. It was the same reaction everyone else made whenever someone asked them the same question. It was against human instinct to say no to the question. It was sort of in the same vane as asking a grown adult how they are doing. No matter what, the answer they will be giving is "good" no matter how dishonest or grammatically incorrect the answer was.

I could see by her smile she knew I had given her the same canned response everyone else gives when faced with that situation. It was as though she wanted to tell me a story that would both frighten and intrigue me simultaneously. She knew I did not want to hear of any of her conquests, but she also knew I would hang on her every word, due to my prolonged absence from her side, and an undying love I was unaware I was capable of before she and I had met. She was mutually benefitting me, and torturing me, and in that dichotomy she found happiness.

"There was a guy, he was always just kind of around, you know?" she said. "He was average height, athletic body, but not really built, you know? More...toned. He had more of like a swimmer's body. The type of body one would imagine Jesus had in real life, when he's all sexy and potentially fuckable. Not the way they portray him in the statues of him nailed to the cross, all skinny, malnourished, weak and what not."

Of all the people in the world I had bound myself to I had found the one who was both complimenting the basis of the Christian faith, while being completely blasphemous in the same breath. She cared not about who she offended, or who she didn't. She probably found more excitement in offending people than she did in agreeing with them. Never did she seem to be a person who just wanted to mind her p's and q's and accept her fate at the hands of what society thought was the correct way for a lady to act, or speak.

"He had this blond hair, that was parted to the side, and after a long day it would fall over his eye making him look very mysterious," she continued. "He was quiet, too. Very quiet. But I would see him out, and he would be fiddling. Always fiddling. Twisting a pen throughout his fingers, or spinning it around his thumb, which always amazed me, and, honestly, turned me on. Or tapping his fingers against his leg, or the bar top or against his glass. He was always fidgeting with his hands, and I noticed he would make origami some of the time."

I looked into her beautiful blue eyes as she continued to tell me her story. I had spent so much time staring into them while she told me story after story before we had taken our hiatus from seeing each other. They still glinted in the light whenever she would peer off into a different direction, sparkling like tiny diamonds, which I found ironic because she hated what people did to get and mine diamond mines. With each passing flutter of her eyes, which often happened as her eyes remained still only when she was talking about sex, all I could think was every kiss begins with Kay.

"Little swans, fish, butterflies, and stuff. He would make them out of bar napkins, receipt paper, the little tabs that held silverware rolls together, or whatever else was just lying around," she said. "He would make them, and then he would just leave them where ever he happened to be sitting. I asked him why he would do that and he said he liked to think someone would pick up the origami and find a little happiness."

Her eyes watered slightly as she thought about him, whoever he was. I wanted to wipe away the tear for her, but I also didn't want to give her the impression that she and I were in a good place, or even that I had forgiven her slightly for what she had told me. I watched as the single tear hung there in the corner of the eye, wanting to fall, but hanging on as though it would perish if it were to fall to the ground.

"He wanted just to give people a little happiness when they

weren't looking for any," she said. "The night he told me that I took him back to his place and fucked him all night long. I figured maybe he needed a little happiness in his life, too."

I looked at her in shock. I couldn't believe she would tell me this story, as though this was some sort of secret I wouldn't have been able to figure out without her telling me. I didn't need for her to tell me she had picked up a random, good-looking, stranger at a bar, I had known that about her past. Hell, I had been that stranger before. That news was neither shocking nor surprising. It was just another thing she wanted to tell me so I would question whether or not I should continue to do so. She seemed to get some sort of perverse pleasure out of telling me things that were meant to hurt me. If I had a best friend, I would be afraid she would tell me she had slept with him at some point when we were still hanging out.

"I don't want to tell you this to hurt you," she said, looking into my eyes, seeing the pain she was causing me. Either that or the connection I wanted to believe she and I shared was more of an actual thing than she I had ever thought truly possible. "I tell you this because I want you to know that in that moment, at that time, I was in love with that guy. But the best way I could ever put it was that I didn't truly love him, in all honesty, I am not 100% sure what his name was, Neal, or something..."

I nervously chewed on the inside of my lower lip, waiting to see what sort of bombshell she was going to drop next. This was the exact type of conversation I would have loved to have overheard while sitting at a bar, and now I was actually in the middle of having one. My brain kept rushing onward to begin to tell the story of what it was that happened next, and how it all played out. I kept having to remind myself this was a conversation I was in, and no matter what my brain said, this was only going to play out how God, Allah, fate, destiny, or the Flying Spaghetti Monster had it planned out.

"It doesn't really matter," she said. "The fact was, I was never really in love with him, I mean, I was...in that moment I was, in a stronger and more real way than I had ever truly experienced before. But I guess it was sort of like how when you hang a painting in your room, and you don't find a stud to put the nail into. The painting is hung, but it is in the drywall, loosely hanging, waiting for the moment to where it would crash to the earth, destroying everything."

She looked at me again; another tear had formed in the corner of the opposing eye. Both hanging on to eyelashes with every ounce of strength tears may possess, not wanting to reach their fate against the concrete floor below us.

"What I am saying is," she continued. "I loved him, but not fully, I guess with him, I only loved him...loosely."

Reaching up she wiped the tears away, tossing them to the side as though they had never really existed in the world, and nobody else would ever get a chance to see or know them.

"But what I've realized recently," she said. "Was that you were the nail in the stud. There is nothing loose about the way I love you. I made a mistake when I tried to push you away, and I regret it every day. That is my secret, that is what I wanted to tell you, I love you. In the most real and impossible ways ever."

My heart began to beat faster, and I felt as though I may figuratively burst from happiness for the first time in my life. I had never experienced something of this nature. No Christmas, no birthday, no surprise from anyone in my past had come close to the feeling of wonder and excitement that rushed through my veins at that moment. I had dreamed about her saying those words, almost those exact words, to me time and time again. I had spent so long hoping upon hope that she would tell me she loved me with everything she possessed inside of her, and now she had. All that she had told me, all that many would have considered problems with her, or her personality faded away into nothing in that moment. I didn't care if she was an alcoholic, sex addict, with dissociative identity disorder. None of that mattered now. She loved me, and I loved her. In a world filled with millions of people experiencing tormented emptiness and voided nights of loneliness searching for solace in-between the sheets with random strangers, or just themselves and their imaginations remembering the last one who was able to touch their soul in the special way that burns an imprint for the rest of eternity, the two of us had found each other, and that was truly all that mattered. I wanted to pull her in close and make out with her as though we were teenagers in public, without a care in the world, only worried about the person connected to our mouths. Instead, I finished my beer, paid my tab with the blonde bartender with the cute gap in her front teeth, and together she, and I left.

24

That night we left the bar where we first met, what seemed like a lifetime ago at this point. It was impossible for me to remember when we had met due to all of that she and I had experienced since our first encounter when I had met her, and apparently Sixteen and I had shared an intimate experience. It could have been last week, or six months ago, or a year ago for all I knew. The time in which she and I had spent together was time where we worked on building something important, something real. Now we had found a moment in time where we could be together, unequivocally. Never before in my life had I experienced feelings of this nature. I never wanted to awaken from this dream I was drifting through day after day, night after night. I knew what I was experiencing was real, but it all made me feel too good for my own mind to believe it was happening. I tried to think about my parents and wondered if this was what it was like for them when they first met, before they had me, and all of their hopes and dreams were crushed beneath the crippling weight of raising and caring for a child. This was what love was meant to feel like, before life got in the way with every little argument that would eventually lead to the downfall of the relationship, and cause another set of broken hearts to never want to put themselves out there again.

While many would have considered our relationship a boring one, since it was mainly filled with sitting on the couch, watching television, and talking about current events, even though she and I disagreed on courses of action to handle the problems of the world, I found myself perfectly content in the simplicity of it all. The moments when she and I would catch each others gaze, and no words are exchanged, just looking into the eyes of the other person sharing all of our thoughts and feelings through the psychic connection she and I shared I understood more about love and life than ever before in my existence. She would avert her gaze, smile shyly, which was completely out of character for her, then look back at me. Then, as though we were incapable of actual speech, she would point to one of her beautiful blue eyes, then her chest around the area where her heart was, and then to me. I would get a smile across the width of my face, shake my head, nervously chew on the inside of my lip as I did from time to time, and tell her I loved her too.

The meetings we went to became the foreplay for our dates. As we listened to the stories of others and their struggles and plights dealing with their addictions to sex and love, we would begin to think about experiencing each other. When it was her turn to talk she began her update in a stereotypical way, saying how many days she had been free from compulsive sexual actions, to which the group would applaud her progress, as they seemed to for everyone there. Then she would continue with how what was going on in her life, struggles she faced, areas she needed to work on in order to not feel tempted, and so on and so so forth, and then she would close her talk with an homage to her favorite author by saying, "So it goes."

After the meetings would end, our most basic wants and needs would take over our better judgment, and we would be entwined within each other as our bodies became one. Every drop of bodily fluids we could share with each other, without crossing the lines into new and disturbing fetishes I was not willing to experiment with, would be shared. Our passion would drive us to make each other cum more times than the other, and as our bodies continued to explode with ecstasy caused by the other I could feel our love growing, and the two of us becoming closer and closer, expounding toward a great and wondrous mutual climax, both figuratively and literally. When our lovemaking was over we would bask in the limelight of the wondrous act we had just completed, waiting for our hearts to finish beating in unison as our bodies and minds cooled to their usual 97.8 degrees. We wouldn't have to speak; nothing ever needed to be said between the two of us. Ours was a world of mutual understanding and exceptional harmony. Never in history had two people been so in sync as she and I were once we had admitted to one another how we felt. Even the most narcissistic of narcissists would look at our love and feel a sense of jealousy, or desire.

Of course, there were nights where she and I could not perform our usual lovemaking. We had to restrict ourselves in order to save her from feeling as though she was about to relapse. The look of fear and confusion in her eyes on whether or not she wanted to do this because she legitimately wanted to, or because it was a compulsive reaction from somewhere deep inside of her to some random event that occurred earlier in the day that triggered some potentially negative feelings to arise within her, was a look I began to recognize early and was constantly keeping an eye our for. I saw myself as not only a lover of hers, but also as a protector and overseer of her safety. I never wanted to be the cause of any sort of hurt, physical or emotional; she may experience in her lifetime. On these nights we would normally find ourselves sitting in our presumably assigned seats on the couch, me on the right side, she on the left, looking ahead, eyes forward toward the television with the blaring noises and lights of one of a thousand movies we may have watched together over the course of the lifetime she and I shared in my head.

Even though it was never expressed verbally I knew on a deeper level she appreciated my candor and respect for her restrictions, restraints, and reservations. Even though for the first time in my life I understood the wants and needs men complained about having, I knew it was better for her, which would, in turn, improve everything between the two of us, if I was to ignore these urges and just be there for her as a friend, as opposed to someone who wanted to just spend time with her on a physical level. This would bring us closer in the areas of relationships in which foundations were laid, giving us a future many could only hope for. True, in the short term it may appear as though the right move is only to show you want to be with a person in a boyfriend/girlfriend capacity as to avoid the proverbial friend zone. In the long term is when you don't end up with the girl because she has chosen another who was there to listen to her, while also proving his worth as a boyfriend, or more. This is when you find yourself alone and left wanting something more from a life filled with hours of masturbation, alcohol, and other forms of self-gratification.

The times that she and I spent on our opposite sides of the couch may not have been the most luxurious or exciting nights, but there was enough going on with us that it was good for us to enjoy a break now and then. It was more than just a boyfriend loving his girlfriend and her loving him back, it was two people who were essentially connected in every possible way attempting to make it in a world that seemed to have had its crosshairs pointed at them from the time they were born until the day they met. True, my life was not filled with the problems she had experienced, and for that, I considered myself forever grateful. My problems all stemmed from the broken psyche I had been dealing with for as long as I could remember. It caused me to live a life inside my head without being able to vocalize any of my thoughts, finding my brain rambling on within itself, getting so wrapped up in tangents I sometimes forgot the thought process that had led me to where my mind had wandered. Sometimes it felt as though I was thinking the thoughts of five different people all at once who were battling with the others on whose idea was the most pertinent in the discussion at hand. I equated it to the feeling I had heard many refer to as being stoned, even though I never truly saw the appeal of the feeling during the few times I had experimented with marijuana in my younger years.

Even though I found my problem to be one of grave importance I could see, thanks to my relationship with her, it was not one of the hardest things people had to deal with in their lives. Unlike so many others who thought the fact they couldn't get past the last level of whatever video game they were playing, or they didn't have enough money to buy the newest and best phone that came out on the market, was the worst thing in life, I had the unfortunate benefit of being able to look at the woman I was in love with and know that anything I may have considered a problem in my life was nothing in comparison to the difficulties she had to deal with on a daily basis. For this, I loved her more, and for that, I was forever changed in ways I would have never been able to explain before she came into my life truly.

25

"A sex addict. What the fuck is that? How the fuck can that actually happen? I mean, look at me. I'm overweight. I'm not attractive. I have this unkempt red beard. I'm not good with people. How does someone like me end up in these meetings day after day, week after week, month after month, looking for answers to those questions, hoping that I won't have an uncontrollable urge to go home with someone tonight, or end up in the barroom bathroom, or the back alley, or the backseat of a car, or anywhere with someone. When did it become something I could no longer control in my life?

"I don't even know how it all happened. I was just like any other high school kid. I went to school. I played sports. I hung out with my friends. In the mornings before school, and at night before I went to bed, I would masturbate. It's what teenage boys do. I would take the Sports Illustrated swimsuit edition and go to town on myself. Either that or I would picture whatever girl I had a crush on that week in precarious positions with my eyes closed, and I would jerk off under the covers hoping to god that my parents or sisters wouldn't walk in. There were times I would sneak off from the Sunday morning sermon and jerk off in the men's room, all those girls dressed in their Sunday best, looking so good. I understood why they used to say showing the knee was inappropriate.

"I guess I should have realized there was a problem when I found myself sneaking off to the bathroom during school just to rub one out. But I just assumed all of my friends were doing the same thing, and it was just something none of us ever talked about with the others. Then I was lucky enough to have sex, with Jamie McCartney.

"That was where everything really changed for me. I didn't care about any of the things I had been raised to believe. I wanted to have sex all the time. Jamie wanted to most of the time, but there would be those times when she didn't want to, and in those moments I found myself going to pick up women at bars, even though I wasn't old enough to be there, I found my way in just long enough to take a woman home. I had no standards, I would essentially find the worst looking one there, the one I assumed would be the most open to the idea to sex with a stranger, get her to take me to her house, or car, or whatever, and then I would go and see Jamie later that night.

"She got so mad when she found out about me doing those things, and I was upset when she broke it off with me, but I guess I understood. I wouldn't want to spend all of my time with someone who would just go out and hook up with anyone whenever I wasn't in the mood, but I'm always in the mood...which is something I am trying to keep under control, and I need to work on that, I can't keep letting that be a portion of my life.

"I don't know; it's hard, you know? I want to be better, but with no sex comes no alcohol, and no public settings, and being alone means no porn, and no internet, and no Sports Illustrated, or any magazine really because I can't control myself whenever I see a Victoria Secret ad, or any ad that has a woman in a swimsuit. I had to get rid of my iPhone; now I have this old flip phone from the turn of the century. It only can make phone calls and play snake. Some girl told me she tried to sext me the other day and it apparently got bounced. Which is good for me in my recovery efforts, but in the real world of business and having any semblance of a social life I am failing miserably.

"I just really want to be normal, you know? I want to be able to take a text from a friend who is asking me to meet him for a beer after work at a real bar. I want to be able to talk to a woman who I am not just thinking about taking to the bathroom to put it in her real quick. I want to wake up and start my day without having to struggle with the thought of 'whatever you do, don't masturbate before you get out of bed.' I want to be able to tell people with absolutely zero shame about where I am going every day. I don't want to hide who I am, and I just really want to be normal. Just for a day, I want to be normal.

"Right now I am on 16 days, and I am really struggling. But I'll be here on Thursday, and I will be at another one tomorrow, and I will find more because I want to succeed. I can't fail, not this time. One day at a time, right? Right now it feels like one minute at a time."

The slightly chubby ginger, with glasses, and bright orange shirt stepped down from the podium as a few people whispered their words of encouragement to him. It was obvious he was in pain at the moment, struggling to make it through yet another day of his own brand of torturous sobriety. I was certain if we weren't in this particular poorly lit room filled with people who preferred to stay anonymous he would be crying quietly, until he broke down and pleasured himself to the first magazine ad for domain name registrars he found. The point of these meeting was to instill the attendees with a sense of hope for the future, that recovery was possible with the right support base holding them up when the nights seemed longer than the days, and the days were filled with nothing but temptation and sin. There were the days where a person like that poor gentleman would speak, and he would lay his blanket of depression across the room. These would make me worry about her, as her struggle grew with every passing day and she looked to me for strength. I would only be able to hope she would be able to find the strength to come to me before she broke down and all of the work she had put in to being sober was lost in a fleeting moment of regret, much like how the slightly chubby guy's night would almost certainly end.

I glanced over at her, and I could see a look of worry on her face, a look I had not seen before. She appeared confident in almost every aspect of her life, even when I knew she was questioning many of her actions, and much of her life, she did so with an air of confidence masking any uncertainty she did not want the world to see. It was strange to see her doubt herself, or her abilities. If she had the ability to doubt herself, it gave me the ability to doubt myself, and with that, I would find myself falling down the philosophical rabbit hole that had trapped so many stoners throughout history.

Am I really who I think I am?

Does she love me the way she says she does?

Do I love her the way I think I do?

Do I really know what love is?

How is it possible she and I were lucky enough to meet, fall in love, and end up together? Is there some grand master plan?

Does God actually exist?

Have I been wrong about so many things in my life leading me up to where I am sitting today?

How did any of us get here?

How was all of this created?

Could we all be just figments of the imagination of someone else, and none of us know the difference between our fictitious existence and the reality of the world?

How many angles can dance on the head of a pin?

10,000 apparently.

I caught her out of the corner of my eye looking at me while I was spiraling downward into mental oblivion, questioning the fabric of all things in existence, and the concern she had in her eyes gave me solace in the fact that yes, our love was real, and nothing about this was fabricated within the boundaries of my head. Our love was going to be epic, and a story I would be happy to tell to people at parties, if she and I were ever invited to parties together.

26

One morning, a while after she and I reconnected at the bar we originally met, and a while before she and I would part ways permanently, I slowly opened my eyes as the sun began to penetrate the tiny slits in the openings between the curtains, illuminating my face and waking me from my slumber. I wiped away the crusty sleeps that had imbedded themselves in the corners of my eyelids and looked over at the woman I was in love with, who had spent the night the evening prior, making it an unknown amount of days in a row that she had fallen asleep with me. I normally awoke before she and assumed I would look over at the peaceful face sleeping next to me once again this morning. Much to my surprise I found her awake and staring at me with eyes wide open and a goofy grin plastered across her face. Only, this wasn't her face; it was a different face, a familiar one, but not hers. I looked into her eyes, and I could see I was looking into they eyes of a different person, they weren't blue like hers were, nor were they green like Twelve's. They were a mixed bag of colors, mostly blue, a little green with golden flecks distributed throughout the iris. The new look startled me noticeably, and the person I was lying next to jumped back afraid and started to cry.

"I'm sorry," the person wailed, as I quickly sat up and covered my chest with the blanket as though I was putting up a thin shield between myself and the person I had found in my bed. "She didn't want to wake up yet, and I had never met you."

Slowly my guard began to drop as I continued to awaken, and I recalled the fact that the woman I called my girlfriend came with other people who had the tendency on occasion to appear when I may or may not be expecting them. Not knowing who it was I was talking to I decided it best to dress myself quickly, not wanting any of them to see me naked except for her. I understood that each one of the "kids," as she called them, was still technically her, but I felt weird for anyone else besides her to see me without my clothes on. I grabbed a shirt from the bedside we had carelessly flung to the side before our passionate lovemaking had commenced, and luckily a pair of boxer shorts were also within arms reach. I carefully pulled them on making sure to not expose any part of me to whomever I was speaking with at that moment. It was a delicate line I knew I had to walk with the kids. I had to think of them as separate people, not extensions of her. I was pretty sure if I were to allow anything to happen between myself and any of the younger ones I would be doing damage to a six, 12, or 16-year-old mentality, not the mentality of the woman for whom I had fallen. I also felt if I did anything with the ones who were of age, even though I had yet to meet them, I would be technically cheating on her, which I never would want to do anyway. For these reasons I had decided I would, within my known ability, not have relations with anyone other than her. She and I had discussed this once, I informed her of my thoughts on the matter, and she had cried saying nobody had ever cared enough before to not want to hurt her or any of the kids.

"I'm sorry," the girl whose voice seemed higher than that of

Twelve said. Even though some may have considered it in poor taste, I had decided to make a game out of attempting to guess which one I was talking to at any given moment. I knew this wasn't Twelve because Twelve would have said hello since she and I had spoken before. I didn't think it was Sixteen because whoever it was said we had never met, and even though I was unaware Sixteen and I had met on a biblical level in the past. That left me with Thirty-three, Nineteen, and Six. Just based on the few words she and I had shared so far this morning I was assuming it was Six.

I assured her it was okay and that I had just been startled, and it was not a problem she needed to worry about. Almost immediately her demeanor returned to one of joyfulness and playfulness. A sigh of relief left her mouth and the smile that had previously filled her face returned. She sat up on her knees and rocked forward and back, just watching me as I moved around the room.

"How old are you?" she asked. "You look like you're older than her, but not by a lot. How old is she again?"

I told Six that I was 33, about to be 34, and that She was 25. Six nodded and playfully bounced up and down on the bed, utilizing her knees as the moving force. As though there wasn't a single care in the world she bounced, not even knowing all of the problems that lay ahead of her in life. She seemed so happy, so young, so innocent, but there was still a darkness lurking behind her eyes. I thought it could be all of the bad stuff that occurred to the others trying to make its way to the surface, or perhaps the secret that caused her to splinter off and create a six-year-old other self. Either way, it was good to see a life filled with hope and ambition. I wished I could change the future for this poor girl, but no matter what she would always be six, and the pain the others had gone through would always be a lasting part of her subconscious.

"That's right," Six said. "I knew that. She's old, but you're even older. Twelve told me you were like grandma old. And that's really, really, old."

I began to wonder if I had been the same when I was her age. I tried to remember if I considered all people, who weren't in my inner-circle of friends, to be old. As I grew, the way I viewed age changed. When I was a teen, the twenties didn't seem that old anymore. Once I made it into my twenties, I looked at thirty similarly to how I saw the twenties in my teens. Now that I was in my mid-thirties, or close to it anyway, I looked at forties as just another time period I would have to live through, and those around me who were around the same age did not look as old as how I envisioned people in their forties when I was a teen, or even in my twenties. Age is a completely relative number, because a six-year old sees someone who was my age, who has lived 550% longer, and the possibility of such a thing seems daunting at the very least. Where someone, like me, sees a person who is forty, and only having a little more than six years left until I am that age, they seem young and vital.

"Twelve says you're really nice," Six said. "Twelve is my best friend and if she likes you than I like you. Nineteen though, he's not nice, and the people he likes aren't nice, so if Nineteen liked you, I don't think I would like you. Most of the people she, dates are people Nineteen likes, and most of those people are, people who like to hurt us."

I sat down on the bed next to Six. Her face was a mixture of happiness, and sadness. The exuberant life that had filled her eyes moments before seemed to have drifted away, hiding somewhere behind the darkness of her unknown future. I was certain she was living with a constant question on why she always seemed so sad. There were many facts about her life she was not allowed access to, or so I imagined. I wondered if she knew that all of the people she talked to and considered friends were all taking up space in the same body, or if to her they were out there among the world, living normal lives. I could see the importance of keeping her in the dark about these things. News like that could shatter her perceptions of reality, and who wants to shatter the perceptions of a six-year old. It would be the same as someone comforting and protecting their little sister, or daughter from the evil that plagued the world. Just as in those situations I felt that Six knew about a darkness that had slowly enveloped her world, and even though none of the others ever told her about the problems they all faced she knew something was wrong, and all she could do was put on a happy face and hope she could make it through the days smiling. It must take a certain level of bravery, and naivety, to go through life unsure of why you never got older, or why portions of your life seemed to be missing, or just a certain uneasiness you would have to live with when lacking answers to some of life's simplest questions. Part of me wanted to protect her from the pain, and I knew I could never tell her about the things that happened to her as she got older. I could never be the one to destroy that innocence.

"Do you know why she cries a lot?" Six asked me.

I shook my head, which was not a lie, but not the truth either. I had an idea on why she cried from time to time, and most of it stemmed from stories I didn't want to ask of her. I was certain she would tell me portions of them as she felt more and more comfortable around me. While some may say that you have to feel 100% comfortable around someone in order to love them truly, I believed it is possible to love someone without wanting to have shared all of your darkness with them. I knew deep inside that this is what she was doing for me. She was protecting me the same way I wanted to protect Six, or Twelve, from what I knew about their lives.

"She cries a lot. Sometimes when it seems like she's happy,

too. It just comes out of nowhere. She'll be like la-la-la-la-la-la," Six said, dancing around on the bed, waving her arms back and forth. "And then she get's all sad and doesn't want to talk to anyone, and she starts crying out of nowhere. I always want to know what's happening but Twelve tells me not to worry about it.

"I guess I'm not old enough yet. I'm not old enough for anything. I mean I'm six, and I've been six for a long time. How old will I have to be before they start telling me things?"

Six started to pout while sitting there in front of me. I understood the feeling of nobody thinking I was old enough to do any of things I wanted to, or know about things I was curious about. Perhaps it was due to so many people telling me I was too young my entire life that I grew up so sheltered and now suffered from extreme social anxiety. I understood the need to keep kids in the dark about things, certain things their brains weren't ready to process, but after a certain point, it causes problems that cannot be undone without the benefit of professional psychiatric help. Six, was in a different situation than I was, but I could still see her point of view. An entire life wanting to know what is happening, but never getting an answer is not much of a life at all. Even if she didn't realize it, she was never going to get older, which meant she was never going to be trusted with certain information. This was a fact she was going to have to live with for the eternity in which they all existed inside one body.

"I'm hungry," Six said. "Can we get pancakes?"

27

Six and I sat in the red vinyl cushions of the plastic yellow seats that lined the tables at the pancake house just off the highway by my house. Even though smoking had been banned in restaurants for years in another overreaching move by the government to control people, there was still the stench of stale smoke clinging to every corner of the building. This was, no doubt from the countless amount of drunks who came in for eggs and carbs to saturate the alcohol sloshing around their stomach after long nights of drinking, while the decisions they made still seemed less like mistakes than they would the next morning. This was where they would chain-smoke a pack of cigarettes while recounting the night in as much detail as their poor brains would allow them to in their drunken state, talking louder than their friends were talking, just to be heard for the first time during the course of their evenings.

The young black girl who was the only one working there during the daylight hours was filled with more joy and pep than anyone I had ever expected to come into contact with at a pancake house. She bounded up to the table with a gloriously large smile on her face, as her pulled back hair bounced playfully behind her.

"How are you?" she asked making direct eye contact which made me feel a little uncomfortable. Even though I knew a normal waitress wouldn't ask any particulars of my life I was unsure of how I was going to explain that I was sitting in the booth with the six-year-old who was living inside of my legal-aged girlfriend because my girlfriend had yet to awaken from her slumber after a night of passionate lovemaking.

"We're good!" Six said with all of the energy and excitement of our waitress. "We're here because we want pancakes!"

"Well it's a good thing you're here then!" the waitress whose name tag read "Nya," said. "Because we have the best pancakes in town."

I knew this was an unholy lie, being that she worked in a generic pancake house, and there were restaurants in the city who had been lauded for their pancakes. Some garnered so much acclaim that unless one wanted to wake up at 6:00 in the morning to get in the line just to get in the door they would never have the experience of going to them. While I had never had the motivation to remove myself from under the covers in order to carb up before the sun was shining, I had heard glowing reviews from many people I could only assume stayed up the entire night rather than wake up a mere amount of hours after going to sleep. I also understood her desire to keep up her jovialness, and for this I declined from asking her if she had ever tried anybody else's pancakes. In every workplace, no matter if the employee loves the job, or despises it, they must hold on to little things in order to get themselves through the workday. It is almost impossible to go an entire shift keeping up the energy and happiness people like Nya exuded on a daily basis. The people who would want to take that from her by injecting their own brand of pessimism into her cheery demeanor were people who hated their lives on such a grand level they had to bring others down to where they were mentally. Essentially they were unhappy and upset about where they had ended up and wanted others to be punished for their mistakes in life. While there were days I was one of those people, I didn't want to take Nya down from her cloud today. Also, I wanted to show Six there were good people in the world, who found contentment seeing other people being happy. Even though I wasn't sure if I would ever see Six again, I wanted to show her I was the good person Twelve told her I was.

"Can we both get an order of three big pancakes?" Six asked, her multi-colored eyes burning with excitement.

"Of course you can, sugar," Nya said. "Anything to drink with that?"

"Two coffees," Six said, which surprised me. Even though Six was living in the body of a 24-year old, I assumed she wouldn't like the taste of coffee. I knew it was a drink many people had to acquire in life, and wondered if over the last 18 years she had actually completed this feat. "And a water, too."

"No problem," Nya said, scribbling everything down in the ticket book furiously, attempting to write as fast as a six-year-old could talk when excited. "I'll be back with your coffees in a minute."

Nya walked away, not with any sense of urgency, but with an air of flight in her step. She didn't walk, but she glided away, almost to the point of floating when she left to get our coffees. This was not the walk of someone who had grown weary of her job, or life in general; this was the walk of someone who had found a happiness within herself that nobody would be able to take away from her. No matter what sorrow happened in her life, she would alway be able to reach down within herself and find whatever seed of joy she had cultivated into an entire persona of exuberance. At that moment I envied her slightly, but also questioned how much was hidden by a naivety toward life. I watched her as she moved around the open kitchen area getting our drinks ready for us, and while she did this mundane task, I questioned whether I would rather be happy or naive, and decided I would not waste any more energy envying her that, or any other, day.

"I don't really like coffee," Six said, looking at me, seemingly knowing my thoughts about her odd choice of beverage. "But if she wakes up and wants some I want it to be here for her. She gets mad if she doesn't have her coffee when she wakes up."

I completely understood that concept. The only thing that could drag me out of bed some mornings was the promise of coffee. I often had fantasized about dating a girl who awoke before I did on a regular basis and would bring me coffee in the morning while I was still in my bed, half asleep. If I was better at fantasizing I am certain she would be a girl in her early twenties, with dark hair and intoxicating eyes, with a butt so fantastic men would envy me for sleeping next to her, who also enjoyed giving filatio, and wanted to ensure I was happy in every possible way every day. Unfortunately, I was not great at fantasizing so the dream of having a girl bring me coffee every morning was the best I could ever dream up. Fortunately for me, I was now with the wonderful, beautiful, amazing girl sitting at the booth with me, and while she may not bring me coffee in the mornings, she was more than I could ever ask for out of my life.

"I like that she hasn't been taking as many baths since you came around," Six said, as Nya, still smiling, dropped off our coffees with little silver pourers filled with cream. "She used to take a lot of baths."

This was a piece of information to which I had not been previously privy. She had never told me about her penchant for taking baths before. I wondered what it could be about taking baths that ashamed her, or gave her pause about telling me. I searched my brain for a reason why she would have liked taking baths, besides the obvious answer of they are relaxing after a long hard day at work, and, more so, why she wouldn't tell me about this non-sexual fetish of hers.

"You don't know about the baths?" Six asked me, seeing the look of confusion on my face. "Even I know why she takes baths, and I'm only six."

I sheepishly shook my head back and forth, admitting to her there was another thing I did not know about the woman with whom I was in love. I wished I knew everything about her, and there were moments I knew more than most ever truly could know about any person who was not themselves, but there were still secrets she was holding from me, just how everyone has secrets they keep from others. No matter how close you wish to be to someone, there will always be a portion of them they leave hidden in their closets, so the rest of the world doesn't judge them poorly.

"When she was younger there was this boy," Six said. "He wasn't a nice boy. He was so mean that even Nineteen didn't like him. Twelve said he was her cousin, or something, but I don't know, because cousins don't do that to cousins."

I already knew what Six was about to say to me. In my head, I prayed to a god I didn't believe in to make it not true. I didn't want Six to say the words I was certain she was about to say, but I knew nothing was going to stop her from telling the one secret she possessed.

"But he made her take baths, and while she was in the baths he would touch her...," Six looked from side to side as though she was getting ready to tell a racist joke. She began pointing down toward her crotch. "Down there. She didn't like when he would touch her there, and I don't blame her, I don't want anyone touching me there."

I could feel myself getting more and more upset, but I knew I could not break down in front of Six. I had to appear as though I was strong and that these facts did not bother me in the slightest, which was a difficult thing to achieve successfully. Every word she spoke drove me closer and closer to anger-induced tears that I knew would stream down my face while I wished I could find all of the people who hurt her, line them up, and shoot them down, without offering them the obligatory cigarette first.

"Whenever he would do that he would whisper in her ear, 'You're dirty, and this is how we make you clean,'" Six said. "She would cry and cry, and beg him to stop, but he wouldn't until he was done touching himself...down there on boys. He told her if she told anyone about him cleaning her she would get dirty again and they would have to do it again."

All of the colors surrounding Six began to turn red. Soon she was the only thing I could see in a sea consisting of Oxblood and crimson waves surging back and forth with every heartbeat that pounded in my chest. It was unacceptable for anyone to have to endure that sort of treatment from anyone, let alone a family member.

"Now, or before you started being here," Six said, smiling to herself, which I assumed was for me being around. She leaned in closely and started to whisper, ever so gently to me, to be sure nobody else could hear what she was saying, "Anytime she felt dirty she would take a bath and scrub away at her body...especially down there."

Nya bounded up the table, hair bouncing every step of the way, holding our plates out in front of her as though they were offerings to the gods. She placed them down in front of us, and carefully straightened them with such care that anyone with a bad case of obsessive-compulsive disorder would have been able to breathe easily.

"Is there anything else I can get for you?" Nya asked, her ever burning smile the only point of joy I had experienced since stepping foot into her restaurant that morning.

I shook my head and gingerly picked up my fork as I watched the large stack of pancakes steaming in front of me, begging for butter and syrup to be smothered and poured over them, just sit there, being pancakes. I forced a half smile as Six picked up her fork with pure excitement, as though we weren't just talking about one of the worst topics any two people could find themselves conversing.

"This is great, thanks!" Six exclaimed, half a piece of pancake hanging from the corner of her mouth, and syrup trickling down her chin.

"Awesome," Nya said before walking away. "If you need anything at all, you be sure and let me know."

I stared at my pancakes, and while I felt like I was hungry, I also questioned how anybody could eat without getting sick due to the ugliness in the world that surrounded them. I wanted to pick up my plate and throw it across the restaurant, hopefully lodging it in the head of anyone who may have hurt another person in their lifetime. Spinning the fork carefully around my thumb I wished I could un-hear what Six had told me, but I knew this was not a possibility in a life that possessed no rewind, nor a delete button. I took a bite of my pancakes, but they seemed flavorless, and bland at the moment I was chewing them.

From across the table, I heard Six eating away, which was interrupted by a slight cough, and a clearing of the throat. I looked up to make sure she hadn't choked by eating too quickly, and for some reason, I was surprised when I saw that I was looking into the blue eyes of the woman I had fallen in love with, and not the multicolored windows to the soul of her six-year-old counterpart.

"I'm guessing you met Six," she said, cutting the pancakes gently with her fork and taking the large syrup covered bite.

28

"You know, I thought this would be easier. I never really thought I would have problems not having sex, you know? I used to drink, a lot. I've been sober for over a year with little to no problems. I used to smoke a pack a day, or more. I quit that on my first try. I used to use heroin. I have been clean from that for three years. But sex, man, that's different. That's a true test of my self-control. You can stay away from bars, and smokers, and junkies, but you can't stay away from people. Even if you do stay away from people we have the internet everywhere, and that you can't escape.

"We all get up here and tell all of us the stories about how we ended up here, going to these meetings, but all of the stories seem to be the same. Maybe not how it all started, I mean some of us ended up here due to terrible things that happened when we were kids, and others of us got here because we had trouble showing people how we cared about them in any other way other than by using our bodies, and me, I only felt like I had any sort of self-worth when I was inside someone else. But we all ended up here because none of us knew how to stop. It's all about stopping, and we can't do that part.

"My friend and I were talking the other day, he has been

struggling with a drinking problem that has cost him more in his life than he would probably be willing to admit, and he was saying he envies people who have the ability to do that. Stopping that is. He wants to be able to go out to a bar and have a drink or two and then go home, but he doesn't know how to do that, anytime he went to a bar, just to grab a beer with a friend, he would get home 8 hours later with little to no recollection of the night, or even how he got home. He was telling me how scary it was to wake up in the morning and not know how he got there, or what he did the night before, but no matter what he had to do it all again the next day. It was a never-ending cycle for him, and that I understand.

"I wish I could just go out and talk to someone without trying to sleep with them. I want to have normal relationships with people, but I can't have those because it's not who I am. My self-worth has somehow become tied to my penis, and I'm not sure if that is something that stemmed from when I was a kid, or if it was just something I was really good at when I was in high school, and I thought the only way people would like me was if I had sex with them. I don't know how I ended up here, but as my list got longer and longer, it surpassed being considered a stud in my friend's eyes, to being considered a sick individual. It got to the point where even I started questioning why I continued to do these things, and suddenly even as I was lying in bed with whatever girl I happened to be there with I was questioning if I was doing her because I wanted to be doing her, or if I was doing her because I wanted someone to think I was a good person, or good at something. Because let's be honest, for those of you who know me know I don't really have any skills, so in order to impress someone I have always felt like I have to make them cum, and I don't want my self-worth to be tied to that.

"It may be too late for me at this point, I don't really know, and maybe it just takes meeting that one special person, but I want it to mean something again. I want to feel like I did when I was sleeping with people I really cared about. I want to feel that connection, not feel like I'm just doing this in order to get someone to like me.

"I remember this one youth group I went to as a kid, back when I was on the pathway to a righteous life, before I realized it was all bullshit, and abandoned the straight and narrow for a life of having fun. But the pastor was talking to us about premarital sex. He started to compare it to fleas in a jar. I don't know if this is true or not, but he was saying that you could put fleas in a jar and put a lid on it. They would jump and jump to try to get out, hitting their heads on the lid. Eventually, they would get tired of hitting their heads on the jar, and they would stop jumping that high. You can take the lid off the jar they would not be able to escape because they would have gotten trained into thinking they would hurt themselves if they jumped that high again.

"I wonder if I won't ever be able to get that close to someone because at an early age I hit my head on the lid of the jar too many times. Now I'm stuck not being able to jump that high and am doomed living a life of being incarcerated in my self-inflicted jar because I am afraid people won't like me if I don't make them cum, and who wants to be with someone whose self-worth is completely wrapped up in that sort of thinking?

"Right now I have gone 13 weeks without compulsive sexual relations with anyone. I still get the itch, obviously, but I'm fighting through the desires and trying to find my own self-worth in myself for the first time in my life. Thank you for all of the support everyone here has given me. It's with this sort of backbone I know it is possible to make it through another day."

Perhaps it was good I was attending these meetings with her. I was beginning to realize my self-worth had become wrapped up in her, which wasn't a terrible thing being that before I had no semblance of believing in myself. Instead of sitting alone at bars and waiting to eventually die, I had found a purpose in wanting to protect her from all of the evils in the world that gravitated to her in a style only she could produce. With all of the stories I heard from her, Six, and Twelve I was beginning to see that some people were just the type of people who attracted evil. Not that she was asking for it to happen, or not that she was looking for it, but she was the sun in a universe of evil, and while everything was circling around her eventually it would make its way into her vicinity, harming her somewhere between slightly, and permanently. I wanted to be a force field, protecting her from all of the meteorites of badness trying to crash into her.

She was stoned faced during the meeting, which was unlike her. Typically she was very animated and excited to hear the people talk about how long they had been clean, and loved hearing about the success stories that were shared with the group. Sometimes though, like today, I felt as though the stories hit too close to home, when she slowly began to realize that possibly her self-worth was too closely related to who she has sex with, and how often she had sex with them. I wondered if she thought I only liked or respected her when we were lying in bed together, in the act of copulation. I wanted to tell her it wasn't about how often we had sex, or even if we never had sex again. My love for her came from somewhere deep inside of me, and wasn't going to expire the day she and I stopped making love with each other, if that day ever came.

Since the diner, she and I hadn't spoken much, which I assumed was from a fear of what may have been said by Six over breakfast. Living in her constant state of uncertainty was something I was sure was a terrifying experience, especially now that she was working on opening up and actually allowing herself to love someone for the first time in her life. It was scary for me to allow myself those types of emotions and to allow myself to feel what I was feeling whenever she and I were together physically, so for someone who had found themselves at these meetings because she didn't know how to deal with real-world emotions without showing them with her different orifices.

Maybe these meetings weren't good for me to attend after all. They were beginning to make me feel sorry for her, and for myself instead of making me feel like I, or she, was able to get through these rough parts together. Even though it wasn't the first time, nor would it be the last time, I was truly beginning to doubt the strength of our relationship. All I could do was hope she and I would be able to weather the storms that rocked our what sometimes felt like an impenetrable relationship.

29

She and I went back to the house, in the moderately bad part of town, but not the worst part of the city, after we finished our coffee, pancakes, and a meeting. We pulled into the driveway, where she stopped right by the door, instead of pulling all the way in like she normally did. I looked over at her, as she stared out her driver side window at the neighbor's cat, Sid, coyly played with a furry toy he had dragged from inside the house. I knew she was upset about disassociating for so long around me. That was a period of time in which she was not in control where I was having conversations with her kids, and she had no input about where the conversation went. She had to fear whether or not Six told me something she was not ready for me to hear, which Six had done, and now she wasn't sure of how to act around me due to her uneasiness about the entire situation. I could only imagine the amount of terror I would be filled with if I had pieces of my life missing, and during those times I knew somebody else was in control of everything I did and said. I would constantly live in a state of fear wondering and questioning. I know I would hate that feeling, so I could only imagine what she was going through, after living with it for so long.

"I know what Six told you," she said curtly, continuing to stare out the window. "She told Twelve, and Twelve then immediately told me. I didn't want you to know those things. When people know those things, they tend to stop wanting to talk to me. They feel sorry for me, and I don't like when people feel sorry for me. I don't want people to feel sorry for me. I am dealing with what happened on my own; I don't need anyone to feel sad because of what happened to me."

I could understand where she was coming from in that sense. I also understood why people did feel sorry for her when they found out about what happened. There is an underlying desire in human beings to want to aid those around them, especially those to whom they feel close. While Six was telling me about the tragedies they went through, I admit, I did feel sorry for them. I also wanted to protect them from others. I wanted to protect them from themselves. I knew that in a world filled with so much darkness and despair protecting everyone from evil would essentially be impossible. I wanted so badly to be able to place an invisible force field around her heart that would activate whenever something bad was about to happen to her. I understood this was less plausible than being able to protect someone from the evils of the world. No matter what I would always wish I could be there for her, to protect her from the world, and no matter what I knew I would always come up short. I would forever long to help her, and she would forever resent me for those feelings.

I wanted her to know everything was going to be okay. I wanted her to know I wasn't going anywhere, not until she wanted me to go away at least, and that was something for which I would never wish for fear of having my heart broken for the first and, presumably, last time in my life. I could feel an emptiness grow inside of my chest as she sat silently staring out the window. Part of me wondered if she was feeling the same thing I was, I wondered if she too was being emotionally paralyzed by a fear of finality between her and I. I had faith in something for the first time in my life, and that faith was in us and our relationship. I knew she and I would be able to make it through the trials and tribulations we faced as long as we both believed in us. That was where the difference between our relationship and God laid. Even if I ever decided to begin believing in Him, I knew He would never start believing in me, and we would never work in any long-term capacity.

"I know this seems like any other typical roller coaster type of relationship," she said, continuing to be unwavering in her concentration of Sid the cat, who now had moved on from the toy he had dragged outside to the carcass of some dead rodent I could only assume Sid had created. "I don't want you to think I'm going to break up with you, and get back together with you, and break up again. I don't even want you to think I'm going to end it with you now, because that isn't what I want to happen. Unless you want that to happen."

Pointlessly I shook my head. She wasn't paying any attention to me. I thought about our relationship and how, even with the strange circumstances surrounding it, I wanted nothing more out of my life. I couldn't have asked for a better person to be sitting in the car with, hoping to all hope we were not in the middle of the last conversation we would ever have. As I thought more about it, I began to realize how often I had already had that thought since she and I met, and wondered how many times was too many for a thought of finality such as that one. While I knew I could promise myself this was the last time I would allow myself a thought such as that one, I knew I was making just another empty promise I would probably have no intention of keeping. It's like all the smokers who promise they will not have another cigarette, or the alcoholics who swear they had their last drink, or the cheaters who promise this will be the last random bar skank they pick up from the bar while their wife, or husband, is out of town. They are empty words with no backing, because in the end, we are slaves to our most basic desires, whether it be nicotine, drinking, sex, or, in my case, her.

"When I was younger I used to dream someone would come and take me away from those who hurt me," she said, as Sid danced playfully around the rodent carcass in some strange feline dance of the dead ritual. "Whenever that would be happening to me I would close my eyes tight and ask God, or Allah, or any of the other deities I had heard of to make it stop. All of that was pointless because it just kept fucking happening. Over and over and over again."

Even with the words of how she didn't want people to feel sorry for her burned into my brain I still felt myself begin to have feelings of sadness, as well as a guilt rise from within me. It was as though I wanted to hold her close to me and tell her I was sorry for all of mankind and all of the terrible things they do to every species on the planet, but most of all, what they had done to her. I could feel the pit in my stomach grow darker and weighed down with the pain and regret she felt on a daily basis. Much like all of my hopes and dreams, I found myself desiring another impossible feat in life, by wanting to take all of her anguish and torment throw it on a bar-b-que, grill it to a nice Pittsburgh rare, top it with Jim Beam steak sauce, and eat it with a side of mashed potatoes, and arugula salad, with parmesan cheese and almonds. Then the pit in my stomach would be justified, and her pain would be gone forever, until I had my morning bowel movement and I would flush it down my toilet, out into the sea, where eventually, one day, it would be consumed by a dolphin, which would then be eaten by whatever asshole or Japanese guy would eat a dolphin, and the pain would then be inhabiting someone who deserved to feel that level of sorrow.

"Sometimes it feels as though you are the one I had been begging the world to send me," she said, finally looking me in the eyes. "Thank you for that, and know that it is just one of the countless reasons I will always love you, no matter what happens with us."

30

Throughout nights and days filled with separate levels of happiness and unabashed worry, she and I rode the roller coaster of our relationship founded on the fact she and I would actually die for other if need be. The times of worry and unsettling lead to times of happiness and joy which hindered completely on how disassociated she had been in any given period of time. The times where I spent more time with Twelve and Six the worse our relationship was as she worried about what they may have told me while she was away. She was always concerned I had met the other three, Sixteen, Nineteen, and Thirty-Three, but as of yet, with the exception of the first time she and I had spent the night together, and Sixteen had her way with me, I had not met any of them. I understood her concern, but based on the information Twelve and Six had given me I would only meet them whenever she was in a truly dark place, and since I had been around, she hadn't been in a dark place, which made me feel good whenever they would tell me that. It made me feel important in ways I assumed would only be topped if she would tell me herself.

The things I heard about the others was mainly negative, except for Thirty-Three. Thirty-Three was supposedly very quiet and kept to himself. There was never a real need anymore for Thirty-Three to resurface, since she never really needed parenting anymore. What I had learned from looking up similar cases online, and based on what Twelve and Six had told me, is each one of the others surfaced in specific situations when she needed that particular personality strength to take over. For instance, Sixteen was more of a protector. Whenever she was about to do something that may be considered destructive Sixteen took over and absorbed all of the pain she may have experienced. Twelve was there to handle any real bouts of emotional turmoil and had been bearing the brunt of arguments and fights ever since she was actually 12-years-old. Six came around in moments of confusion, which apparently happens during periods of sleeplessness and whenever there were too many drugs or alcohol introduced into the system. Nineteen was the destructive one. He was there to take over whenever it was time to hit the proverbial self-destruct button on life. According to the others I did talk to his only hope in life was to one day be able to say he was the reason none of them existed anymore. He didn't want to live anymore, for a reason unbeknownst to me, and the only way to be successful with such an endeavor was to either commit suicide, or convince one of the others to kill themselves. According to Six, he had come close once or twice in the past. It was terrifying for me to think someone could have that sort of power while living inside, and feeding off of, the person he was wanting to end. He was the dissociative parallel of an endoparasite, with the desire of completing his life-cycle by brining an end to all of theirs.

"He's scary," Six has said to me on more than one occasion.

"He yells a lot," Twelve told me here and there and also said he reminded her of a man who used to come around when they were all living behind a church. He was nice when he was around other people, but when it was just the two of them, he would get a lot louder. She told me how he would yell at her and tell her to do things she didn't want to do. When I asked her what sort of things he would ask her Twelve's eyes filled with tears and her lip started to quiver.

"He told us to take off our pants," she told me. "He told us to take off our pants, and then he made us lie down on the couch. She would beg him to stop. She wanted him not to touch her with those things but the more she cried, the more he yelled, and that made her cry more. Nineteen makes us cry when he yells, and then he yells at us to stop crying, so Six, me, and Sixteen cry more. Then I remember that guy whenever he yells at us like that, and I cry more, and then Nineteen yells more. It's scary, and it never seems to end."

The conversations I would have with Six and Twelve would slowly begin to paint me a picture of pain and sorrow, worse than any words I could conceive to type here today would ever be able to convey. They would tell me with child-like innocence about the atrocities others had perpetuated against them as they all grew up together. Most of the time one of them would come to the aid of her, in order to protect her from the full brunt of the agony one would feel, but this was not always possible. On occasion, it was so dreadful that not one single individual would be able to handle the full load, and they would pass it out among the multitude of those who were dwelling within the confines of the skin of this one person. Each story they told me weighed on my soul as though I too had experienced the darkness. While I would never have admitted that to the woman I was in love with, nor to those who also occupied the body within which they all survived, each and every time they recounted one of the tales of child molestation, and rape committed against them I felt a piece of me die, and even though the memories were theirs, and theirs alone, I almost felt as though I could envision the atrocity as though I was there, experiencing it with every ounce of my being.

Never before meeting her, and all of those who came along with her, had I ever been so overcome with the desire to cry not only for the strength of one individual, but also for the lack of humanity and justice, which now plagued human-kind. When people wondered why more and more people had stopped believing in the Judeo-Christian idea of God I now had the answer. This was one of the answers the truly hard-core religious would respond to with answers such as, "God has a plan," or "The devil has workers out there around the world doing his bidding, also." When there was no answer those answers were acceptable to anyone who had the ability to think freely about what in this world is right, and just. The irony of it was if any of them had experienced an iota of the pain she had gone through, or just the tiny amount she had allowed me to be exposed to, their faith would be shaken to the very core. Although they, as with most people who hate to have their faith tested, kept themselves guarded from these sort of happenings, denying these sorts of people exist in the world, or at least denying they exist at the level in which they do. They are the people who can't believe they would have a gay relative, and would rather deny the most basic of instincts to people they care about most by saying they are making the choice to be despised by peers and relatives just to make a point of some sort. They are the same ones who can't believe their brothers, daughters, sons, fathers, mothers have done unthinkable things in the past, more afraid to admitting they were part of a bloodline where someone would have committed a heinous act, than to concede some people are just bad people with impulses that got the better of them. They would sooner blame a victim than to accept their friend actually committed the crime of which they are accused. Denial was their best friend, because denial allowed them the ability to continue to believe in an almighty, omnipotent, and just God.

Every time I looked at her I knew there was no such thing in this, or any other, world.

"Are you okay?" she would ask me whenever she would come back from an extended period away where I had been blessed with the company of Six or Twelve, rather than hers. She would know what we talked about, and the look on her face was always one of terror I may decide to stop loving her for what I had found out. I would nod, and smile, knowing I couldn't stop loving her for any of the things Six or Twelve had told me. If anything I would feel closer to her, with the hope that one day I would be able to protect her from another one of these atrocities before it actually occurred.

31

"It started out innocently enough; I just wanted my friend to be my friend still. I thought if I didn't want to have sex with him he wouldn't still like me. So, we were at his house, and he started telling me that he wanted me to take my clothes off, but I told him I didn't really want to, and he got this look on his face. It was a look I can't ever forget. It's the same look so many guys get on their faces whenever someone tells them they don't want to have sex with them. It's not anger, or sadness, really. It's more of a look of dejection.

"You have to be watching closely to see it, because they all try to hide it. They never want anyone to know about how they are hurt because someone doesn't want to be with them. That look gets me every single time. They quickly mask it with either anger, or apathetic insolence, but if you look closely enough, it's there. Something about that look makes me want to make it all better. It makes me want to be there for them. I think it's because I know I caused that pain in them. I made them feel like they were worthless, and, let's be honest, all of here know what it feels like to have someone make you feel worthless. I don't want to do that to them, so I almost immediately change my mind.

"Then we are there, on the bed, together, and he asked me

if he could do something to me...he wanted to stick it in my ass...and I told him I didn't want that, and he gave me that look again, and I felt like I had to give him that, I had to let him know I didn't think he was nothing, so I let him do it. And then he came. He came in my ass with absolutely no warning, and I didn't want him to, but he didn't even ask me. He just did it, and then he rolled off of me, and rolled over and grabbed his pants. He told me I should leave, and the face he gave me that convinced me to sleep with him, and to let him stick it in my ass, was the one I was certain I was giving him, but he didn't care. He told me I had to go because he had 'stuff to do.'

"So I left, and he barely walked me to the door, and didn't even kiss me goodbye, or anything. He didn't really care it was my first time. He just wanted to tell everyone what had happened, and he did. He told everyone we knew, and soon all of my friends who were boys were calling me because I was the girl who would let them do anything, and I did, because I wanted them to like me, but I didn't really want to.

"All my girlfriends stopped talking to me, and even talked bad about me behind my back because I had done all of the things with their boyfriends they weren't willing to do with them. None of the guys wanted to date me, because, I mean, what would everybody say? Nobody can date me; I'm the girl everyone has already had. Anytime I started to get close to someone they would find out about everyone I had been with and they would leave me, but then one of their friends would suddenly be calling me because they wanted to have a turn with me. What am I supposed to say? No? I can't say no to one of them, because what makes him different than any of the other guys I had already been with? What about that would be fair?

"I tried moving; I tried leaving it all behind. But somehow, every time, someone would find out about who I am, and what I had done, and the next thing you know I would be sitting there next to one, while another one was hitting up my cell phone looking to do everything they had ever wanted to do with a girl. I could never escape the person I was trying to forget I was.

"Luckily I found this group, and now I know I have the confidence to say no, and even though every day is a struggle I know I have the support of a lot of good people who want to be there for me, and who don't want to sleep with me, or use my body as a playground for all the rides they never took when they were young.

"I can say I'm 84 days sober, and I love every minute of it. I don't know where I would be if it wasn't for you all in this room, I really don't. Thank you, to each and every one of you. You are all amazing in your own individual way. I always thought that whole 'one-day-at-a-time' thing was bullshit, but it's not, for all of you new people in the group today. Trust in your self-control. You can make it through the night without issue. I promise. Look at me. I did it, so can you."

The musty, poorly-lit, church basement back room echoed with a smattering of applause from the addicts who were more than half-listening as the speaker moved her way down from the podium. The people who spoke on a regular basis at the meetings she and I attended seemed to be sincere in what they said, but the cynic in me forever thought they were just spewing the same garbage so many others did in order to make a minority of people feel good about their lives. While I would like to think the anonymous brunette speaker who looked vaguely like Audrey Hepburn after a rough weekend in Vegas was honestly on 84 days without compulsive sex, I wouldn't bet on her to succeed if she had to take a phone call from one of her male friends tonight. I hoped Audrey wasn't lying because I would hate to know that nobody was successful in their quest for sobriety.

I looked over at her and saw there was a tear clinging to the corner of her eye, as though she had been reminded of a moment or two from her past. I wanted to wipe it away for her, hold her close to me, and let her know I would never be the type to let her down by using her for her body and then leaving her there, naked, cold, and alone. I also knew it was not the wisest of moves to express feelings of attraction or love while sitting in a room filled with people who were addicted to acting on those feelings. The last thing anyone in that room wanted was for my innocent act of affection to spiral out of control into a full-blown orgy in the basement of the Evangelical Free Church on 5th St. The way they talked about triggers and having to be careful of acting on your learned desires in these meetings it seemed as though this was what they were most worried about occurring, rather than having an entire group of addicts have to start over at day 1 again.

Every meeting we attended I longed to end. I wanted nothing more than to be away from these people. I didn't judge them, nor did they depress me in any fashion, but my foray into the world of addiction to self-gratification was short-lived, and while I was definitely not the norm in this room, or any other room for that matter, I felt as though I had been cured when I decided it was time for me to stop relying on others to make me happy, and I searched for happiness within myself. Those days seemed like ancient history to me now, and I know they ironically ended when she and I found ourselves once again tangled within each other's limbs, but I felt as though I had found a minute amount of inner-strength within myself. Within my happiness, I found strength, within strength I had found self-control, within self-control I had found a desire to protect and take care of her. Unfortunately, unlike the other members of this group I found myself in, my strength had the possibility of wavering if she and I were ever torn apart again. Their strength was being built from meeting to meeting, with personal victory, to personal victory, and mine was all riding on hers and my relationship, and every meeting we attended reminded me of the fragility of the bond which connected us.

This was why I found myself rooting for every single person in this room to succeed, but cursed them when they failed, for they had filled me with doubt about not only myself, but also she and I.

32

She had been searching for something her entire life. It was something intangible, and something of which I was truly unable to provide her. No matter how much I wanted to be there for her, to be the cure for whatever it was that ailed her I knew she needed something more out of a life that had been so sun-drenched with trauma she suffered from a form of cancer that couldn't be cured by injecting poison into her veins, or visiting a shaman in Northern Asia. No her disease was deeper than in the organs or blood of her body, it was in her soul and no matter how many times I told her I loved her, or promised her I would always be there for her in her time of need, I knew she needed more than what I was offering, much to the point that upset me when I thought about failing her in that way. Instead I knew she had to find this solace somewhere I could not be, she had to find it somewhere deep within herself, and I obviously, being a socially-inept person with only one friend, with the ability to make up entire worlds in the caverns of my mind was not the right person for that job. So I was less than overwhelmed with joy, and not at all surprised when she told me she had begun to see a new psychiatrist, Dr. Hager-Allen.

"He truly is a brilliant man," she told me once she admitted to seeing him in the hours she and I found ourselves separated. "He's been helping me a lot with a lot of the issues I have...including, you know, the kids."

She told me about her sessions with Dr. Hager-Allen and how they talked about the different trauma that occurred over the course of her lifetime. She said they discussed all of the things I had learned about from Six and Twelve, and a few things I had yet to learn. Her sessions had apparently been aiding her with not so much as dealing with the trauma that occurred and the negative reactions to said trauma, but learning to deal with it in a healthy and productive way instead of having compulsive sex with strangers, or significant others, or allowing the dissociative breaks to take over in the cases where she is in a situation where she found herself about to relapse and needed to guard herself from her surroundings. It was going to be a long road to a full recovery, according to her, and there may never be an end to that journey, but it was the help she was looking for, and was a great and wonderful compliment to all of the support I had provided over the course of our relationship.

We sat on the light-green couch, and I watched the light dance in her blue eyes while she talked to me about the good doctor, and what their shared goals were for her recovery and what the first steps were for her, lined out by Dr. Hager-Allen.

First: she had to stop using, taking, drinking. However, they were administered, any and all mind-altering drugs. This included, but was not limited to, any drug on the Food and Drug Administration Schedule-1 list. So that meant no more smoking pot, no more cocaine, no more heroin, in any way these drugs would be taken. I knew she had been sober from many drugs since she had left rehab, and even though I wondered if she had smoked a little pot while she and I had parted ways, I was relatively certain she and I had never spent time together whilst she was under the influence, with the exception of that first time, where technically I was being courted and engaged with the company of Sixteen, and not her.

Also in this step was her exclusion of alcohol from her life. I knew how difficult of a thing it was to stop drinking, even though I had never considered myself an alcoholic, and I knew she struggled with it on a daily basis. Many people feel as though rehab is a magical place that allows you just to stop using whatever your drug of choice is once you have stopped using it for four to six weeks. The truth is, it is a constant struggle. They say one day at a time in the SLAA meetings, just as they do in AA, NA, etc. because it truly is a struggle for one to wake up day after day and make the conscious decision to not drink. It's not just a matter of not buying a beer, or not going to a bar; it is a complete and total life adjustment where the alcoholic constantly has to remind him or herself that the next drink they take could be the one that kills them. There is a saying spouted off by those in recovery to remind themselves of the dangers of drinking, "One is too many, and a thousand isn't enough." This is a mantra spouted off to give them strength when they are thinking what the harm may be, where the danger in one beer, the possibility of a relapse from one vodka, the odds that this one glass of champagne is the one that begins the slow, torturous route of alcoholism into the cold, steely hands of Death. I was unsure if she had experienced her own relapses over the course of our relationship, but she had kept them hidden from me, I always assumed she had broken down a few times, because we met again after our hiatus at the bar in which we met, and I was never sure if it was her breath or mine, but I could have sworn I smelled light beer.

Second: she was being urged to avoid all places that could be considered triggers to the trauma she had experienced in the past. This included all bars, night clubs, discos, churches, and bathtubs. While I was unsure of why she was asked to stay away from all churches I assumed this was a story, I would eventually hear later from one of the kids, assuming this therapy wouldn't immediately make them disappear from her life, as well as mine. I understood the train of thought on this request by the doctor. Anywhere she may visit that triggered any recollection of her trauma could, in turn, have her relapse hard into a plethora of problems. I knew this was for her safety and I wanted the best for her, so I was on board with the plan of action the doctor had set forth for her to follow.

Third: she was to avoid any and all romantic relationships with anyone.

She began to cry as she spoke the words to me. I couldn't tell if she was crying because it broke her heart, or because it broke my heart, or because it broke her heart to break my heart, but I knew all three of the scenarios were coinciding at that very moment. How was it she and I were going to proceed? I had felt as though throughout most of this relationship I had accepted a lot from her, and dealt with it with a smile on my face and a forgiving ear for almost everything she had to tell me. If we couldn't make love one night because she was afraid of it rehashing trauma she had experienced when she younger, I obliged and never said a word about it. I was completely on board with the complete and total lack of drinking she and I practiced, or at least that I practiced since I knew about her problematic lifestyle when it came to alcohol. Even though I never found myself in need of going to an SLAA meeting, or any meeting for that matter, I went with her to show my support, because that is what a boyfriend who cares and loves their partner does. While much of my life, or the lack thereof, had been turned upside down by the inclusion of her in my life I hadn't complained to her once. I wanted to show her I was an understanding, caring, open-hearted, open-minded individual who wanted to be there for her in every way possible. The fact that this new Dr. Hager-Allen wanted to take that away from, not only her, but also away from the man who felt and desired all of the things he felt and desired for her, and she was just going to go along with his recommendation even though it was obviously breaking her heart to have to pull the trigger was where I was going to have to draw the line in our relationship. It may have been considered selfish by the doctor, or by her, or by a multitude of people looking on from the outside, but from my perspective at that moment I was the only one who was being punished for there for a person and wanting to help in her recovery in a healthy and positive way.

"But don't worry," she told me as she wiped the tears away from her eyes. "I already decided I was just not going to tell him about our relationship. I will one day have to tell him the truth, but I'm not ready for this end. Not yet."

33

"Not yet." That was an interesting choice of words for one to choose when describing their desire not to have a relationship terminate. If she would have just ended her thought two words earlier than what she did I feel as though I wouldn't be wrapped up in my head wondering why those were the words she chose. While I understood that obsessing over words such as those was stereotypically something overly attached teenage girls did, and not really something men who were 33, not quite 34, were prone to do, but I found myself wondering why she had phrased it the way she did. I would have asked her at the moment if I hadn't been overtaken with joy that she was deciding to stay with me rather than to take the advice of her doctor. Once the joy wore off and I had a moment to think about what she had said I realized she had given our relationship an expiration date in her head, and while she may not have known the exact date she and I would part ways, it was obvious she was already looking toward a future in which I was not involved.

I walked the cold, rainy Nashville streets with my hands in my pockets wondering what it would taste like to smoke a cigarette so I could turn my misery into a stereotypical photograph of loneliness and angst. My breath could be seen hanging in the air directly in front of me as I walked around the neighborhood that was pretty bad, but not the worst, thinking about when the other shoe would drop, and she would no longer be saying "Not yet," but instead would be saying "Now." I felt the light rain hitting the top of my head, rolling down the nape of my neck, and gently gliding down my spine sending a chill through my entire body that was similar to the feeling I had experienced with our conversation only a few hours before.

If I had been a stronger man, and not a man who relied on the make-believe world he created in his head to get through years of loneliness, I would have just decided to end it with her then, but I was not that man. Being relatively unexperienced in relationships throughout my life I had occasionally wondered how I would react in situations similar to the one I was currently living. In my head. I always had the bravery to walk away, the strength necessary to say goodbye, and the fortitude to stand by my decisions. As I had been learning throughout hers and my relationship, though, I was not the man I dreamed of being while I was battling the nights by myself while I was looking for a reason to wake up the next day. I wished I had that strength though. I wanted to be a stronger man. I didn't want our relationship to end, but if it had to I wanted it to end and for me to walk away with my head held high, never looking back, always looking forward to a bright and happy future where I would have learned from the experiences of my last relationship, and not holding on to them like so many people did with their pasts. I didn't want to become the equivalent of the former high school jock who constantly talked about his glory days on the field, while he was never able to reconstruct these moments in the world when it counted. I was afraid if she and I went our separate ways it would be the last, and first, relationship I would have ever been a part of in my life because I would forever be too afraid to venture out among the world to see if I could find someone else who made me feel just a fraction of how good she made me feel.

Walking from street to street, down the tiny strips of concrete and asphalt I hoped no intoxicated driver would be venturing down, I just thought. I thought about my future, I thought about our future, I thought about her future without me, I thought about how long of a future I would have once she dropped the axe and cut me out of her life, either on her own accord, or on the recommendation of the quack, Dr. Hager-Allen. I wished I had another friend in this world I could go to for advice in this situation. A male friend who I could ask his opinion on her use of the words "Not yet" as opposed to just not saying anything, and then I could take his suggestions based on his past experiences, relationships, and lessons learned and not follow any of them, and mildly resent him for recommending I end it with the woman with whom I was in love. He would, of course, understand my resentment of him for these reasons, because that's what friends do for each other, and he knew if he had ever come to me for advice in the same situation and I had given him the same words of wisdom he would resent me for them as well. Alas, I did not have that friend, nor any friend I could sit down with and talk to about my issues in relationships. I was navigating this ship through a storm completely blind, only hoping she would be able to right the ship before I lost all control and we went down to our watery deaths with everything on board, metaphorically speaking of course.

My hoodie had become damp with the rain that had been stinging my face for the duration of my walk. I could feel the chill penetrating my blue, V-neck T-shirt and inhabiting my skin in a way that could only be described as invasive. I wanted to be home in my bed, with her, where I wouldn't have to worry about any of this, but I knew that was an impossibility due to the fact the words were already out there in the universe, floating around my head like birds around the head of a cartoon duck who had just comically fallen down the face of a mountain hitting his head a few too many times before landing on the rocky floor with an audible, and painful "Thud."

Instead, I found myself walking around the neighborhood, hoping I wasn't going to get jumped, or worse, for the $12, the pack of Blackjack gum, and the phone from the turn of the century I had barricaded in my pockets. I wasn't even carrying my wallet on my person that evening, which wasn't that much of a surprise because I never carried my wallet on me anymore. There wasn't much of a need to carry one. I was old enough as to never get carded whenever I was frequenting bars, and I always had enough cash on me to pay whatever bills I was going to have to settle up. For instance; tonight I wasn't going anywhere, and would not have to pay anybody money for their wares or services, so I only had a few dollars on me, left over from earlier when I had to buy gas, the $12 change from my two twenties I had on me. If I were to be going out to a bar or restaurant for dinner I would be carrying considerably more on me, hoping that my tab, and obligatory tip, wouldn't exceed $60 American, no matter what country in which I found myself.

In *The Divine Comedy*, Dante adorned the doors of Hell with the phrase "All Abandon Hope, Ye Who Enter Here" in order to allow those who were banished to eternal damnation that the only thing that could make the torture worse was the hope that one day it would all come to an end. This was how I was going to have to enter the next chapter of my relationship with her. I knew it was going to come to a heartbreaking and terrible end, in my eyes anyway. The worst practice I could subscribe to was hoping she would see that I was a healthy alternative to any of the guys out there in the world who would only see her the way she thought they saw her; an object to be used and thrown away as though she was a tissue, or paper hand towel one gets from the restroom at a rest stop on a highway to a final destination.

Hope was a promise of the omnipotent gods, and while I didn't believe in gods or devils, I did believe hoping was just as dangerous in believing in an omnipotent being who had a promising and rewarding future mapped out for believers. Either way, when life doesn't work out, you are left alone, more hurt than you began, because the randomness of life cannot fulfill the promises both hope and gods make to those searching for answers in a world filled with none.

34

How many television shows could two people watch in silence before it became completely and utterly obvious to the both of them there was no future between them? The apparent number, based on how many shows she and I watched, was infinite because when you're in love the obvious problems plaguing a relationship can get lost in the mundaneness of procedural television shows where the criminal is usually the second one accused and has already been let go, or the character inexplicably helping the police find the killer. It is simpler to focus on these fictitious issues and problems rather than look inward and work up the courage to discuss the problems occurring within a relationship head-on. The longer you kick the can down the road, the harder that can will be to repair, but the option is an easier one when faced with a dilemma that will probably conclude with the termination of the relationship. Out of everything she had taught me about women, about caring for others, about respect, about love, I knew I would remember that allowing yourself to love someone completely, allowing someone else into your heart, your mind, your soul was a gamble. With all true gambles there was always the chance someone was going to get hurt, and in the case of broken hearts, there were increased odds more than one person would have to suffer the consequences of a person's careless heart.

I could tell she felt it, as well. There was a divide between us, and even though I attempted to hide this from her until I could figure out a way to rectify the situation myself, I could feel her pulling farther away the longer I sat in silence about what was weighing heavily on my mind. Disguising problems such as these from one's significant other was futile as the energy being put off by the one in a negative headspace will be picked up and carbon copied by the other. There will always be the questions being asked and suspicious statements being made silently by the one who feels the trepidation of the other. "What's wrong with him?" "Why is she acting weird?" "He's being a little mean today." "She's being a lot quieter than usual." "He hasn't wanted to sleep with me in days." "She hasn't told me about her day once this week." "All we do is watch TV." "All we do is go out." "Why does he want to hang out with our friends all the time now?" "Why does she suddenly want to go out with her friends every night?" The list of worries goes on for an unprecedented amount of time in one's head, trying to figure out why, what, when, who, or how, when the answer typically rests in the person sitting next to him or her, or, more realistically, within themselves. Pushing the problems farther down the road, hoping that one day a bandaid would be invented to fix the geyser of problems exploding from the sanctuary of trust they have built their relationship on, the wounds continue to seethe every ounce of brilliance the relationship once held.

I could see in her eyes the confidence she once had for our future had faded, and with every moment where I didn't bing up the problems was another moment where her faith waned more. Soon they would be entering into the new moon phase of her own personal relationship cycle, hoping to capture the brilliance and awe of the full moon she and I once shared.

"I was talking to Dr. Hager-Allen today," she said, her eyes never averting from the television, even though nothing was on other than the annoying insurance commercial with the spokeswoman who had been hanging on for years past when she was relevant, or remotely funny. "He was telling me I needed to attempt to assimilate myself into the normal world. Ever since rehab, except with the short amount of time you and I spent apart, I haven't been out there in the world. He feels as though it is a good idea for me to try to go out into the world. Start out a little easy. Find my comfort zones. Not jump right into anything too drastic, but see what I can find out there to do, so I'm not always cooped up, hiding from the outside world when there is an entire world out there to explore."

Assimilate. It has many definitions, none of which I had ever been a big fan, but the ones mattering most in this instance were "to resemble" and "to bring into conformity." He was telling her to resemble the normal world. I didn't want her to resemble the normal world. Neither one of us are accepted by the normal world, so why would it be something we would ever want to resemble? For a person who was so strong, and so confident in who she was I was surprised she found the idea of following a patterned world from her throne on high straight into the gates of hell an appealing one. This was something so very out of character for her, and maybe this was all part of her new recovery, or maybe this was her way of telling me she was going to be slowly pulling away from me. Either way, there was nothing I could do to stop her.

"I think I should probably start by going out and finding a job, or something, you know?" she said, asking a question that was obviously more of a statement than anything else.

She didn't want or need my opinion. She never asked for it, or needed anything of the sort from me. "I think maybe if I can find a job around some like-minded people I can find another level of happiness."

I knew what she was saying. She wasn't saying she was unhappy now, she just thought, like most people, that there was more out there in the world for her. The problem was, when most people went out looking for happiness aside from what they have already they typically tend to lose the happiness already stored in their wallet, comfortably hidden in their back pocket along with the one zinger they hold on to in case of an emergency that requires a well thought out insult, and the name of the person they wish they were sleeping with instead. My problem was I held all of my happiness out in front of me. I didn't store it in my wallet, or backpack, or any other personal carrying device, because all of my happiness was found within her.

I know so many people say it is imperative to find happiness within yourself before seeking a relationship with another person, but the truth is some people just have that personality that cannot be happy on its own. This is obvious in any number of cases where an outgoing and happy person who is just burdened with too much life for his, or her, hometown moves to another area. In the days, weeks, months, or years where this person is working on finding a new group of friends to associate with, they can feel the darkness begin to take over their body. It happens slowly at first, inching under the skin of the newly plagued, dragging them down each passing day, as they long for their old home, their old lives, their old worlds, but know they can never return for fear of the laughter and comments that will most assuredly be snickered behind their backs by the number of people who never had the guts to leave home and hated the ones who left for shining a huge, blatantly obvious, spotlight on their own insecurities about how they had too much fear to do anything with their lives except for breath. The sorrow becomes common-place, and soon they long for the last of their own breaths...until they finally find a group who accept them as their own, and happiness has been achieved within the boundaries of a group of people.

We had found that special brand of happiness, or at least I had. I wanted to tell her I disagreed with the idea, but I knew she wasn't going to want to hear that from me. A needy, jealous, controlling boyfriend I did not want to be. This would only result in fights I would not win, and only the small amount of hope I carried for our relationship would begin to disseminate quickly. I looked over at her as she remained motionless, watching the blinking lights and heard the blaring sounds coming from the television propped up in front of the two of us with not even the slightest bit of concern of how I may feel about the decision to trade her self-imposed incarceration, for a life of social acceptance among the world.

Her eyes reflected the lights of the television, and for the life of me, I could not tell what color they were at that very moment.

35

Perception is a strange thing. One man's viewpoint of a situation can be completely different than another man's, while a third may see it in a completely different way. There is the age-old adage about relationships: there's her story, his story, and then the real story. While I was certain her story differed from mine on so many of the details I assumed there were some points that could not be debated. This included our "meet/cute," our reuniting after time apart due to life getting in the way, our first fight, our first breakup, our reuniting after our first breakup, and even though I wasn't sure, I assumed she was also slowly realizing she was not in love with me as much as she had initially thought she was. There wasn't a whole lot to be said once someone comes to that realization. She would see me more and more as a person who she cared for, much like a distant family member who showed up to the major events, and never really caused problems. Slowly she and I would fade out of each other's lives, and while it would take me much longer than it would her to get over our relationship in the end it would probably be for the best, at least for her, and in all honesty that was all that truly mattered. I would slowly learn how to talk to others, just how I learned how to communicate with her. I was almost to a point where I was ready to make that leap the last time she and I parted ways. I would only need a slightly stronger push to get me to the point where I would be able to sit at a bar, drinking my Bud Light, watching SportsCenter, and talk to the person next to me about the top plays and why number one shouldn't have been considered number one, over number three. I would one day be able to look at a girl and say something, even if it takes all of the guts in the world, like, "hi," or just introduce myself to her, hoping against all hope she wasn't a girl who had been to rehab for alcohol, sex addiction, or had the burden of multiple people living inside of her.

I looked at her and smiled. Out of the corner of her eye, she looked at me, and a slight smirk crossed her face, as though she had a secret I didn't know just yet. I chuckled slightly to myself as I remembered the days, which seemed to be so far in my past at this point, when I would become mildly short of aroused at the potential of figuring out a secret being held be someone around me. The stories got me through the darkness that was my life. I was in desperate need to find something to latch onto in order to make it to the next day. Now I had found my strength in being a person, a real person, who did what comes naturally for so many, I was caring for another human being. No amount of over-imagination would ever compare to the natural high I was receiving from being there, and knowing what real love felt like, for someone else. With every passing day, as her recovery continued to approve her quality of life, I could see I was a part of that, and I was there as a catalyst for her actions. I had been a friend, a support system, a lover, and a significant other over the course of our relationship, and all of that was much better than any sort of make-believe story I could have come up about her within my head when she had initially spoken the words at the bar that night.

"Can you keep a secret?"
"Can you keep a secret?"
"Can you keep a secret?"

It was music to my ears for more reasons than I could ever explain to anyone who would be willing to listen. Even to this day I found the syntax and rhythm of the words just rolled off the tongue, and briefly for a moment I wanted to go, disappear in plain sight of hundreds of strangers, and quietly wait and listen for someone to speak the words that would give my sudden desire to live out a story in my head slight reprieve. She struggled with her own brand of addictions, and I struggled with mine, although most wouldn't consider mine to be any sort of life-threatening problem. Only I knew the severity of the issue. Only I knew that getting lost in a world where you are in complete control leads to a god-complex that could only be understood by a complex god. Many may have referred to me as socially-inept, or cripplingly shy, while only I knew I just felt as though I was in control of everything, and all of the people around me were nothing more than puppets for my amusement. They were plebeians who were forced to do my bidding, and none of them ever truly realized the power I held. I had been an all-knowing, all-powerful being, and I knew the problems that sort of power held. It was a boring, lonely life, and while so many longed for that kind of power, I knew it was better to sit on a couch and be grateful for the few moments in a life one could spend with a person with whom they were in love.

I saw as she shook her head, diverting her attention from me, back to the television where basic and simple storytelling was occurring in the form of a TV crime drama with people who were too pretty to be cops were catching people who were too pretty to be criminals in a city where the lines of right and wrong were blurred to an obnoxious state of grey where nothing was concrete, nor intangible. It was a world of moral questions with no answers with people blaming laws for the problems, and never blaming the offender. In a world such as that there would be no real law, it was a world where the problems that arose were not the fault of anyone, and everyone was a victim. A world where everyone blamed others for their problems, and society had more to apologize for than the people who were committing crimes against it. I hated these shows, because I believed in taking responsibility for one's actions, and not wanting the world to feel sorry for anyone who wanted to blame anyone, or anything else, for their short-comings. Sometimes an asshole is just an asshole. There is no need to try and figure out why this is true. It's similar to trying to figure out why some people are genuine masochists. I had read an article once about a guy who enjoyed wearing a male chastity. This device was made up of two separate, but equal, cages, one to constrict the testicles from moving, the other to ensure the shaft doesn't grow beyond it's usual flaccid state. The purpose of the device is to keep people from thinking about anything that may turn them on. If they begin to get turned on the cages cause moderate to severe pain and the thoughts of sex begin to wane as the pain increases. Unless one is a masochist and they enjoy the pain, which would cause the wearer a strange enjoyment, turning them on more, causing more pain, causing more enjoyment, causing more pain. It's a fact of life, and there is no need in questioning why, it's just something that is better to know exists.

While I knew she enjoyed escaping into her television based world of make-believe where the bad guys go to jail, the good guys go home at night, and in between there is nothing but a large, dense grey area, I no longer could escape into mine, because my world of make-believe was an unhealthy escape from reality. Her's was a much more socially acceptable escape. Society had become adept and numb to binge-watching television shows, and writing it off as a day of relaxation that was deserved. The biggest lie we as humans have ever been taught is we deserve something. Advertisers, and marketing companies have worked overtime to instill this belief into our brains, and we have glommed onto it like leeches who wanted nothing more than to buy the newest and shiniest television, so we can sit on the couch and watch 13 hours straight of whatever show we can stream from the internet, all while having somebody bring us food right to our front door. The secret so many knew is we, as humans, do not deserve anything, but will utilize anything in this world to make our lives less active, creating further generations of lazy, entitled, boring people who need to get out there and spend more time getting vitamin D.

"You already know," a voice came from somewhere deep inside of her interrupting my thought tangent, ripping me back to reality. I looked over at her, still staring at the television, coy smirk on her face. There was something different about her, something...new. I was unsure as to what it was exactly, but I could tell there was something unusual with something about the way she looked.

She looked over at me; her blue eyes seemed to pierce my soul with a level of anger and hatred I had never experienced in my world before.

"You already know she's leaving you soon."

36

"You're going to be gone soon," the voice crackled out of her in a guttural and typical fashion of a 50-year old smoker who had sucked more dicks in a lifetime than ten or more women could have ever imagined. I had never heard the voice before, and while I stared deeply into the eyes of the woman I was in love with, I could see they weren't the same color blue I had grown so accustomed to over the course of our relationship. These were lighter, paler, more of a sky color. These were the eyes that could only be carried by one with the stereotypically given title of a "Crazy Girl." Whoever it was talking to me from behind these eyes hated me already, even though, in my world, we had just met. "When you're gone, I will be happy, because you are just like the rest of them. You're all the fucking same. It's all about me, me, me. There is no need to worry about anyone else's feelings. You just come in and take what you want with no concern about anyone else, and then you leave...you, sir, are as much of a dick as the rest of them."

I knew this wasn't Twelve, or Six; this voice was filled with hatred for all things living, filled with a spite that could only come from years of constantly being let down, abused and told there was nothing that could be done about it. The vengeful look that leeched on to my soul in the center of my body and pulled it out through my throat as it clawed the entire way at my esophagus to stay where it had inhabited moments before. I feared it was Nineteen, and he was finally showing himself to me in one last grand action before he would slit both wrists and let all of the people I cared about in this world die right in front of me.

"You, you are just so dumb," she went on to say. "You have no idea what is happening right under your nose because you are too far up your own ass to see anything that doesn't directly involve you. It's no wonder she is losing all interest in you. You are the most narcissistic one of all. It's not all about you, and you will never see that because you honestly believe that anybody else gives a shit about you, or your problems. They're not even real, you dumb fuck. You are such a joke."

Never in my life had I been saddled with the label of a narcissist. I spent all of my time by myself, not because I didn't enjoy the company of other people, but because I literally had no idea how to talk to another person besides her. The only person I had spoken to in longer than I could remember had become more important to me than almost anything else in the world; this was not the action of a true narcissist. I believed the person talking to me may have only recently learned the word as an insult and felt the need to use it at the first possible moment. This wasn't the action of a person in their thirties, or even their twenties. Someone who was nineteen must already know the term narcissist, or so I assumed. No, this could only mean that I was being berated by Sixteen, the angry, angsty, teen with a chip on her shoulder, with good reason, and an infinite hatred for all things male, at the time.

I felt the need to apologize to her, but I didn't know for what I would be apologizing. I wanted to tell her I was sorry for everything that has happened to her, but she had probably heard that story before, and nothing good ever came from empty apologies in my opinion. I looked into the pale blue eyes and could feel the hurt plaguing the mind of the girl who had seen more pain in her short lifetime than most should feel in two, or three, or an infinite amount of lifetimes. I wanted to help her, and tell her I was different than the others, but she had probably heard that story before, and nothing good ever came from empty promises in my opinion. I wanted to tell her that even though she hated me for being male, I loved her for being a part of the woman I was in love with, but she had probably heard that story before, and nothing good ever came from empty admissions of love in my opinion.

"I have seen this all before. I know exactly what you're thinking. You aren't the first, nor will you be the last to come around like you're some sort of savior," Sixteen went on to say. "You're all the same. You feel like you are white knights on white steeds coming in to save the day — which is also racist when you think about it — trying to fix all of her problems as though you can actually change anything. Nothing ever changes. All you know how to do is hurt her and make her feel like she is nothing. I won't let you do that to her. She is too important to too many of us in here for me to allow you carte blanche when it comes to her feelings and psyche. You are just another flash in the pan. You may have been here longer than some of the others, but you won't make a difference in the long run. You're too old, too ugly, too dumb, and too fake."

My entire knowledge of teenage girls came from comedy movies from the turn of the century, and she seemed as though she was nothing more than a stereotype of all of them conglomerated. Her insults were puny, angry words with little backing or knowledge, based on an assumption of human reactions of the worst put downs known to a teen. Old. Ugly. Dumb. Fake. Simple words that would shake the core of someone who had poor self-confidence, but she was talking to someone who never cared about aging, or being considered unattractive, or less intelligent, or fake. I had never worried about these things because I knew who I was, and that was all that truly mattered. It was sad to see her attempt to break me down because she had been broken so many times, and I knew the only way to gain her trust was to allow her to insult me, to try and hurt me, to call me every name under the sun, while never allowing her to see me falter. Then she would see I was unlike the others. I was a force to be reckoned with, and I was there to protect her, not hurt her, or the others inside her.

She continued to spout off monosyllabic jabs and barbs at me, waiting for me to come back at her with my brand of anger, but what probably should have been known to her by now, was I didn't ever truly express my anger outwardly. I would walk away from a situation before I ever allowed myself to say something mean, hurtful, or demeaning to another person who was angering me personally. While I did not disagree with the "Eye for an Eye" doctrine, I typically felt it was better to walk away from a situation before I said or did something I would regret one day in the future. This was just a personal belief, not something I thought nations should practice - nor did I agree with the preemptive strike philosophy practiced by many foreign policymakers in the world, which apparently Sixteen did. Battling against her would be an unfair fight for me to involve myself.

"You can't even say anything back. Can you?" Sixteen harped. "That's because you are just a little pussy boy. An old, dumb, pussy boy. You probably don't even really like girls do you? Would you rather be sucking on some big cock? Or maybe you would like a cock in your ass? When you and her have sex does she take a dildo and shove it up your ass? Do you like it when she does that? I bet you like that, you old, dumb, faggy, pussy boy. You sucked in bed too, you two-pump chump. Probably because you liked having sex with boys and wished I was a boy instead of a girl. I've slept with 12-year olds who were better in bed than you, you shitty fuck."

I stood there silently, watching her slowly break down as she hoped I would say something back, defend myself against what she was saying to me. Her anger intensified, then began to fade, waning more and more by the minute. Each insult thrown my way was another declining moment in her hatred for me. It didn't matter how boring, mundane, simple, stereotypical, ignorant, her insults were, I was going to wait her out, knowing she soon would break, and as her anger shifted to sadness, she began to cry, and collapsed into my arms, tears streaming down her face, and snot running from her nose. I gently held her, being cautious as to where my hands were. I did not want her to mistake any sort of comforting I gave her as an unwanted advance, or inappropriate action. Her body seized with sadness as she gasped for breath in-between her physical and audible sobbing. I hoped she knew everything was going to be ok, because I wasn't going to let anything happen to them, not again.

"Why do we always get hurt?" Sixteen sobbed, her tears staining my shirt. "Why doesn't anyone want to love us? It hurts so much. It hurts all the fucking time. I can't take this pain anymore. I don't want to feel this anymore. All of this is too much. I'm only sixteen."

I lightly patted Sixteen on the back. She needed to get it all out, and this was a good way to just that. I had always found a good cry to be quite cathartic. The sadness and sorrow continues to grow and spread like a terrible STD in a group of open and close swingers, and a few minutes of ugly crying is like the shot of penicillin needed to restore the balance in the body.

"Please tell me this will be ok," Sixteen begged. "Lie to me and tell me everything will be ok."

I wanted to tell her I knew everything would be alright, but I never wanted to lie to Six, Twelve, or Sixteen...any of them actually, even if any of them wanted me to, and I was already terrified how all of this was going to end. Sixteen seemed to have an idea of how this was all going to play out and I was pretty sure she wasn't predicting a picket fence ending with childlike laughter and puppy dog breath.

37

Dr. Hager-Allen had become a permanent pillar in her life, which made him a permanent pillar in my life since she was such a big part of my life, and who I had become over the course of our relationship. I had never met the man, and I had no inclination to do such a thing, but I did not like him. I felt as though he was attempting to change too much, too quickly in her life, and even though I was not a doctor, or even taken a psychology course; I suspected he was increasing the chances she may have a relapse, causing her more problems in the long run. This would require her to continue to see him for a longer period of time, meaning more money for him. While he was trying to cure her, he would be able to abuse the power of trust he held over her, getting her to perform tasks that could potentially act as a trigger, causing her to relapse, and BAM, another couple of years worth of sessions and the house is paid off. Obviously, I didn't trust the man, and was wary about anything he recommended to her. I was certain she understood my feelings about the subject matter and probably attributed it to me being over-protective significant other who was upset by the fact the good doctor's first recommendation was for her to end her relationship with me. This was not the reason I disliked him, and he was probably the one who planted that seed of insecurity in her, which was now sprouting in me. So. Fuck him.

I would seethe in silence as she would prance around my house talking about all the good he had done for her since she had begun going to him.

"He's really turned things around." "I'm really beginning to learn how to control when the kids come out." "Since I've been seeing Dr. Hager-Allen my compulsive need to act out physically with people has really diminished. I can't remember the last time I felt overcome with an uncontrollable desire to have sex." "Dr. Hager-Allen is a genius. There hasn't ever been a man in my life that has had this kind of positive impact on my life."

I understand that people speak in hyperboles. It's a condition, and they don't think about it while they are speaking. This is the best burger in the world. He is the funniest man on the planet. She is the most beautiful woman I have ever seen. That is the best, greatest, most amazing, awesome, shit I have taken in years. They are words, that is all, and to most people, words have no meaning. There is no weight in the vocabulary of most. They are just stringing together the 25 words they utilize on a regular basis to describe their days, and no thought goes into what the effect of those words could be. Did I know she hadn't been experiencing a compulsive need to act out physically recently? Of course, which to me meant she no longer wanted to act out physically with me, because we hadn't made love since she had begun her sessions. Did I know she was learning how to control the kids? Of course, because, other than the episode with Sixteen, I hadn't seen the others in quite some time, and as odd as it was to miss the people living within the body of the woman I was in love with, I wished I could talk to Twelve, or Six again. Was Dr. Hager-

Allen the only man to have that sort of positive impact on her life? I hadn't known her for her entire life, but I felt pretty confident in saying that at the time she and I had known each other I had a positive impact on her life. For her to say otherwise was something being said strictly because she wasn't thinking about the power of her words, and obviously wasn't thinking about all the good I had done for her. So, again. Fuck him.

"I don't know if I would have ever gone out to find this job if he hadn't pushed me to look for something to do," she said. Her blue eyes, her's, not Sixteen's, sparkled in the light with a happiness I wished I had been the cause. Her smile stretched across her face, and she didn't exactly glide across the floor, she more bounded from spot to spot as though she was teleporting through time and space, fueled by her own happiness and energy. "This is exactly what I have been needing. And I've finally got friends again."

Her arms raised in gratuitous praise to a god in which I knew she didn't believe. She looked truly and unabashedly happy, a look I wasn't quite sure I had ever seen on her face before. I chalked it up to my brain intentionally forgetting all of the happiness and joy she had expressed over the course of our relationship so I could justify the jealousy I was feeling at the moment over things that probably didn't make a difference in the long run.

"There's this girl, Kelly," she said. "She's so cool, and pretty, and amazing, and awesome, and...just...I really think she is going to become a very important part of my life, you know? You know, how sometimes you just get those feelings about people and you just know, from somewhere deep within, you know that someone is going to be a part of your life in some facet, and it's just...karmic destiny."

Hyperbole. It's defined as an obvious or intentional exaggeration, but it seems as though it is used more often than not unintentionally. Whenever a person, especially one who doesn't believe in such things, speaks of karma, and destiny, describing each other, to say the least, you know they have fallen into a world of exaggeration from which they cannot escape. The lies have sunk in as deep as they possibly can and are clinging on to the core, deep within a person who is usually so articulate and educated with her responses. She had lost all grip on her reality, lying to herself about her happiness, escaping to a world in her head where all of this was going to turn out perfectly, and without the benefit of talking about life truthfully and realistically she was stuck searching for convincing words in the typical dictionary of the unintelligent, hanging their hope sadistically on whatever lies they tell themselves so they can sleep at night, avoiding nights staring at the ceiling while they slowly realize their lives are completely and utterly worthless. She was becoming one of the masses. She was losing her intrigue. Her appeal. Her worth in the eyes of so many people was dwindling and now, using hyperbole, she was over-compensating for a boring life that would never leave her fulfilled, but was probably a much safer, and conservative route.

"She is just so pretty, and so funny, and I can tell we are going to be best friends," she went on to say, not realizing I had mostly stopped listening, or realizing I had stopped listening but was talking only to hear herself talk so that way she would feel important in her own mind. "I haven't felt this way about someone since I was in grade school, you know? He was a guy who lived a few houses down from me. We used to hang out at his house all the time while his parents were gone. We would play video games and eat ice cream and whatever. We were really close, you know?

"We stayed friends through elementary, and middle school, and most of high school," she continued to tell me her story, even though I knew she knew I wasn't paying much attention anymore. "He stood up for me when some bad stuff happened when I was 16. It wasn't my fault, but nobody at the school cared. He stood up for me in front of everyone, and I knew he was my true friend.

"That day he made me have sex with him, and stuck it in my ass, and it hurt, and I cried. He told me he wouldn't have had to stand up for me if I wouldn't let people do that stuff to me," she said, with a slight look of reminiscing on her face.

I snapped back into the real world, my attention grabbed by the end of, her story. I looked at her, looking at me. She wasn't happy. She wasn't upset. She was just sort of there, looking at me, looking at her.

"Oh, good," she said. "You were listening."

I nodded, shocked by her approach to get my attention, wondering if any of it, if any of this, any of our relationship, any of our conversations, any of this world, was true.

"I'm going dancing with Kelly, and some other people from work tonight," she said, turning away from me and walking down the hallway to get ready. "I don't know if I'll be back."

38

"What the fuck?" the tall, skinny man, with an appropriate amount of scruff, and wild, dark hair splayed out in every direction. "I never thought I would ever get to the point where I would be here, standing in front of a group of people, talking about how I got involved in this group. A sex addict...a mother fucking sex addict...a few years ago I was considered a stud, now I'm a pariah with a problem. How did this all happen?

"I was the first of my friends to lose my virginity. I was young, 13, or at least, that's what I considered young, most of my friends didn't lose theirs until they were at least 16, some of them even later than that. I always thought I was just proving to everyone I was straight. I was this amazing person with amazing abilities. I could have sex with every girl, every girl in the whole world, as long as I was smooth, and nice, and acted like they were the entire world. It didn't matter that I knew we weren't going to see each other again after that night...except at school, or work, or whatever. I mean, I may have lead them on, but I didn't mean to make them think there was a future for us...you know what I mean?

"It was a normal thing; I just had sex with women. I didn't really think about it. But then came the drug use, and soon came the hard drug use, and then came having to pay for the hard drug use. I was marginally employed — if that — and I started breaking into places to steal things to pawn so I could pay for my habits. Who cares, right? It was a victimless crime, most of the places I robbed had insurance, so they weren't really losing anything, other than piece of mind. I would pawn the stuff, take the money to my dealer, buy enough crack to get me through, and the next day do it again. I knew it wouldn't last forever, but I could at least tell myself I was going be ok forever.

"Of course, that's not how life works for most of us, especially any of us sitting in this room today. We never just have our little indiscretions and get through them unscathed. No, we have to travel through hell in order to come out on the other side. So, of course, I went to jail, and then that's when the problems started.

"As you can all see, I'm a good-looking guy. It's not a bad thing. It's gotten me through a lot of difficult situations, but jail wasn't a good one. I could try to lie my way through, but that usually ended poorly for me, so in order to survive I knew what I was going to have to do, even though I didn't want to do it. I found a guy to, essentially, protect me, and all I had to do was have sex with him whenever he wanted. He had been in for a while, so he wanted it...a lot. I mean, a lot.

"If we were out in the yard and he wanted it, I had to give it to him. We were in the showers, and he wanted it, I had to give it to him. We were in the library, or the chow hall, or the bathrooms, or wherever, he wanted it, I gave it to him. But he protected me from the other few hundred other prisoners who wanted to take me the way he would. I guess I just sort of started relating sex to survival. So when I got out 18 months later, thinking I would forget about everything that happened in there, chalking it all up to doing what I had to do to get by, I started going a little crazy.

"I kept feeling like I was in dangerous situations, probably because of the life I lived before I went to jail. That sort of life just breeds paranoia and contempt. Whenever I started feeling like my life was in danger, even if I was in a completely safe setting, I would have to have sex with someone — anyone — and I would look and search and try to find someone to help satiate these urges I was now struggling with. Again, I'm a good looking guy; it didn't take me long to find someone, I just struggled with it until I did. The moment I would get off, I would feel a thousand times better....safer.

"I don't know how this happened, I guess none of us in this room really know how we all got here, but we're here now, and all trying to better ourselves so we can get through the next part of our lives...alive. One day at a time. One fucking day at a time. I don't know how some people have done it for so long. Today I start over, last night I started getting scared again while I was out with some friends, we weren't drinking, there were no drugs, there was no reason for me to feel the paranoia I was experiencing which scared me more than almost anything else. I found this kid, this little kid...couldn't have been more than 18, if that. We had sex in the bathroom at the park, down by the Parthenon, and I felt better. But now I have to tell you, my family, I fucked up, and I have to give you my chips back and start over again.

"I wonder if I'll ever be able to forgive myself for allowing my life to end up where I am now."

I sat there in silence as the other members of the group applauded a smattering of applause, showing their support for the poor guy who was obviously lost in a banal sea of confusion and sorrow. Would forgiveness be possible in a world where I was born broken, put together, then smashed again by her, when she got bored and found my bizarre and odd quirks to be more boring and commonplace than someone of her past and stature was used to dealing. I wished there was a way for her to forgive herself, and for us to stay together, but unfortunately, I was not the type of person she was looking for. She needed someone stronger, someone braver, someone not me. I knew what I was going to have to do, just as I was sure she knew what she was going to have to do.

39

A knock echoed through my house. The repetitive banging on my door startled me as I was awakened from the hour or so of sleep I had been experiencing only a moment prior. I threw on a pair of dirty shorts that were crumpled up next to my bed and staggered my way out of my bedroom door, down the hallway and to the front door where the knocking continued to penetrate my home. I swung the door open to see her standing there. She looked distraught. Something had happened. Her mascara was running down her face. She had obviously been crying. She was having trouble catching her breath. Her lower lip was quivering.

"Can...can...can," she stuttered over her words. "Can I come in?"

I held the door the entire way open and motioned for her to enter. She quickly rushed by me. Her hands holding her jacket close together in the front in a feeble attempt to shield her from any dangers in the world. She sat on my couch, keeping her jacket on, crossing her arms across her chest and rocking back and forth slightly as she stared into the darkness of my living room at 3 o'clock in the morning. Her eyes were vacant. Her full lips remained pursed even as they violently shook below her nose. I walked over and sat down next to her. I wanted to console her. I wanted to protect her from whatever had her scared. I wanted to be the man in her life to keep her away from all of the dangers in the world. I would be much more effective than the jacket she was currently relying on. I reached out to place my hand on her shoulder, to let her know I was there for her. She pulled away and glared at my hand as though it was a ghost from her past before I could manage to touch her.

"You are the most wonderful person I have ever met," she said, not looking anywhere near me, her eyes darting from left to right, up and down, focusing on nothing in particular but avoiding one spot, in particular, me. "I love you, and if I could, I would stay with you for the rest of our lives."

My heart leapt as all of the worry and fear I had been feeling seemed to dissipate immediately. I had wanted to hear those words from her for so long. With all of the hope and promises I had made myself about not succumbing to the dangers of hope I had carried with me over the last few weeks, or months, or years, or however long it had been since she first said the two words that filled me with dread, "Not yet," I was filled with a soothing joy, because I knew she wanted to be with me, forever. I hadn't felt this good since the first time she I had said she loved me. I couldn't explain the sheer amount of happiness that flooded my body at that moment. I could tell something was bothering her, so I attempted to hide the smile that wanted to explode across my face.

"I love you," she said again, still looking away from me. "I love you so much, and I told you at the beginning I would hurt you. I knew I would do something that would ruin all of this. I never wanted to hurt you."

I reached out again, but again she pulled away. She shook her head slightly, letting me know she didn't want me to be near her at the moment. She was not happy with something she had done, and was plagued with self-loathing at whatever happened earlier in the evening. I pulled my hand back, looking at her with genuine concern. I let her know she could talk to me about anything. She just shook her head back and forth, and cried.

"I can't," she said. "I can't. I don't want to remember. I can't remember."

I stood and walked in front of her, kneeling down to look her in the eyes. The beautiful blue eyes I would get lost in time after time. The blue eyes that had a sea of stories to tell with every passing glance. The beautiful blue eyes that at that moment were filled with fear, terror and hurt. I extended my hands, so she knew I was there if she needed me, and I always would be. She looked down at my hands and then lowered her chin all the way to her chest. She stayed with her head bowed for a few moments before she looked up again. I leaned back. She was gone again.

The big green eyes looked around, slightly scared, unsure of what they were looking at, or where exactly they were. Slowly her hands released the grip from her sides, and she looked at them with the big green eyes. Her hands were white from holding on so tightly. She slowly played with them for a moment until the color had returned to their natural pinkish hue.

"Hi," she said, her voice now a few octaves higher, with a childlike quality to it.

I waved back. I wasn't sure which one I was talking to. I was pretty sure I wasn't talking to Sixteen. The anger wasn't in the eyes as I had experienced it before. There seemed to be some sort of recognition in the eyes when they saw me, so I didn't think it was one of the ones I had never had the pleasure of meeting. That meant I was talking to either Six or Twelve.

"She's really scared," she said. "Really scared. Nineteen is mad about something that happened."

I chewed on my lip as she spoke. I knew Nineteen was the violent one. She had told me that Nineteen had no problem causing her harm. I needed to find out what had happened, but I didn't know who I was talking to, or even to broach the subject.

"Do you know?" she asked. "Do you know what happened?"

I shook my head. I wished I could just talk to her, instead of one of "the kids." It would have been an easier conversation. The kids were there to protect her, and even though they said I was nice, and a guy they could trust there was still an amount of skepticism on whether or not I would be someone they could truly confide in.

"It's not good," she said. "Six doesn't even know about it."

I now knew I was talking with Twelve. That made the conversation easier.

"If Six comes out, you can't tell her," Twelve said. "Six can't find out. It would hurt her too much."

I nodded. I understood the potentially damaging effects of telling bad news to a child. Even if the child was trapped inside of the body of the woman I was in love with.

Twelve put her hands up against her ears and shut her eyes tightly. She shook her head back and forth and clinched her lips tightly.

"Nineteen wants to kill us all," Twelve said. "He keeps saying it's his turn to take over. He is just going to end all of us, so we don't keep getting ourselves hurt. Why do we always find a way to hurt ourselves?"

She looked at me with her green eyes. Questions of a child searching for answers I didn't have seemed to jump out of them, slapping me with a face of disappointment. I wanted to tell her everything was going to be okay. I wanted to tell Twelve that as long as I was around no one was ever going to hurt them again. I wanted to tell all of them I was there to protect them from every evil in the world. I wanted to tell them I would make sure they would never cry again, but I knew it would all be for naught. I would have no control over the outside world, and since she still couldn't be in a relationship with me, I couldn't protect her as fully as I truly wanted to. I asked Twelve to tell me what had happened.

"She went dancing," Twelve said. "With Kelly. And a couple of guys from work decided to come with them. She didn't drink though. I promise, she didn't drink. She still is sober. I promise. I really, really do. Do you believe me?"

I nodded. A knot was growing in my throat. I was terrified of finding out about how this story would end. I could feel the butterflies in my stomach taking off as I waited with anticipation for Twelve to finish telling me the story.

"Good," Twelve said. "I like that you believe me. I wish all guys were nice like you. You don't want to hurt her. I like that about you."

I forced Twelve a smile. I knew I couldn't push the subject, I had to let Twelve tell me the story on her own terms, if she felt like I was pushing she would clam up, or worse, she would let one of the others out, and I would have to start from the beginning with letting them know I could be trusted.

"She really didn't drink," Twelve said. "She was drinking water from a bottle, because she was dancing so much. She was hot and wanted water, so one of the guys, a very frat-boyant guy, Angelo, I think was his name, went to get her a water."

I knew the guy Twelve was talking about. He looked like a cartoon version of a mafia member. He was loud, obnoxious and unintelligent. I had seen him around town; I even remember hearing a secret of his once. His fantasy ended with me murdering him.

"And then," Twelve said. "Well…I don't really know…it all kind of…um…I…"

Twelve lowered her head, so that her chin was tucked into her chest. I shook my head. She had become so uncomfortable with the conversation she had gone away. She regressed to the inner sanctuary of the mind. I didn't know who was going to be coming out next, even if anyone would come out, or possibly she would just fall asleep and awaken in the morning feeling out of it and unsure about where she was.

40

Slowly her eyes reopened. They were now a mixture of green and blue, and filled with fear. Not the fear of someone who was afraid for her life, or was afraid of what might happen, but the fear of someone who was unsure about what was happening in her life. Her jaw quivered violently, and tears started to fall from her eyes.

"Hi," she said, her voice even higher than Twelve's was, and sounding ever more youthful.

I knew right away I was talking to Six. I waved to Six, attempting not to show any disappointment I never got the full story out of Twelve before she went away. According to Twelve, Six had no idea what had happened, so she wouldn't be able to help me find out what happened. The only bright side was I wouldn't be able to break my promise to Twelve by telling Six what had happened.

"Are you mad at me?" Six asked as she started to cry.

I shook my head. I could never be mad at Six. She was still filled with an innocence I had lost years ago and desired to get back. She reminded me of a simpler time in my life before I had gotten weighed down by the complexities of life. My life had been nothing like the life she had gone through, and I understood why she wanted to shelter Six from the horrors this world had to offer.

"I don't want you to be mad at me," Six said. "Please don't be mad at me."

I assured her I wasn't mad at her. I was mad at the situation. I wanted answers. I wanted to know what had happened tonight. I needed to know what was going on. I couldn't do anything to protect her if I didn't know what has happened in her life.

"Everyone is yelling," Six said, covering her ears with her hands. "I think we're going to die."

I shook my head. I let her know that no one was going to die that night. I was there, and I wouldn't let anything bad happen to her.

"What happened?" she asked. "No one is telling me anything."

I shrugged. I had no idea what had happened. My mind was racing with possibilities, each scenario worse than the one that had preceded the last. I wanted to give her answers, but there were no answers for me to give her. All I knew how to do was tell her everything was going to be okay. Another lie we tell each other every day in an attempt to ease the pain of living.

"Do you know?" she asked.

I continued to shake my head. I wanted her to stop asking me these questions. I didn't like not having an answer for Six.

"No," she said, annoyed at me. "Let me finish. Do you know what happened to me?"

I looked at her confused. Obviously, if it had happened to Six it had happened to all of them, but to when was she referring? Was this something that happened tonight, or when Six came about? I shook my head, looking at her with concern.

"You can't tell anyone," Six said. "I mean anyone."

I nodded, promising her I would keep the secret between

us.

"My cousin was babysitting me," Six said. "And we went to 7-11 to get Slurpees, and took them back to my house."

I continued to look at her, watching the woman I loved telling me a story about her past through the eyes and the mind of her at the age of Six. I knew whatever Six was about to say was going to be heartbreaking and one of the most difficult things I had ever heard, but I didn't want her to feel like I wasn't interested in her story, but I also didn't want to hear whatever was about to come out of her mouth for my own protection.

"We were drinking our Slurpees," Six said. "He finished his and told me to come over to him. Then he took the Slurpee straw. You know, the one with the little spoon on the end…"

I nodded. Tears started to build up in Six's eyes again. She wasn't enjoying the memory she was telling me about. I told her she didn't have to tell me any more, but she shook her head as she sobbed.

"Well, he told me to take off my pants," Six said, crying over every word. "I didn't want to get in trouble, so I did it. I don't like people being mad at me."

I nodded. I knew this about her. I felt a pain shoot through my heart, even though the logical minded side of me knew the heart had no pain receptors. I was afraid for Six at that moment. I never wanted to have to deal with a memory such as the one she was reliving at that moment.

"He took…the straw, the end with the…the little spoon on it," she said through broken sobs and flowing tears. "And he made me let him…he made me…he…he put it in me…and it hurt…and I cried…and he told me not to, but I did, and he got mad…and…and…"

I gently took her hand in mine. Tears had started to well up in my eyes. I wanted to take her pain from her. I wanted to take the pain from all of them and have it hoisted upon me so that she would never feel any sort of pain again. I wanted to accept it as my own, so I would be the one living with the nightmares, and the constant fears. I wanted to be able to sacrifice every ounce of happiness I had to allow her to forget every bad thing that had ever happened to her, so she could live a life in which she didn't have to be afraid of every guy in public. I wanted to save her.

"Are you mad at me?" Six asked. "Please don't be mad at me."

I shook my head. I wasn't mad at her. I wanted to hold her, to console her. I wanted to protect her from her memories. I wanted to save her from something that was impossible to be saved from.

"It hurt down there so bad," Six said. "I hurt so bad for days after. I wanted to cry, but I didn't want to get in trouble. I thought I would get in trouble if I told. I was told not to tell. He told me not to tell."

I wanted to find her cousin and damage him in many ways. I wanted to teach him a lesson about how to treat people. I wanted him to pay for what he had done to an innocent little girl. I wanted him to realize that if you abuse your power or your responsibilities, there would be consequences you have to face. I wanted him dead.

"Please don't be mad," Six said again. "I didn't mean to make you mad."

I let her know I still wasn't mad at her. I didn't know how else to tell her I wasn't mad at her. I just wanted her to be safe. I wanted to make her life better at that moment. I wanted to exact revenge on anyone who had ever done anything to hurt her.

"Can you tell me something?" Six asked me. Her voice was filled with fear and questions about what was happening. Six didn't know what was happening in her mind. Six had no idea why everyone was yelling in her brain. Six didn't know why Nineteen wanted to kill everyone. Six only knew something had happened and no one was telling her anything.

I nodded and looked up at her, fearing the question she was about to ask.

"Why does it hurt down there now, like it did back then?" Six asked, before she started to break out into a coughing fit, I recognized as Six going away and soon I would be face to face with the woman I was in love with. My brain was slowly processing everything I had just learned, and tried to figure out the answer to Six's final question, when she looked up at me with her blue eyes.

"Did they tell you?" she asked, looking afraid.

41

Rage built up inside of me. I couldn't believe what I was hearing. I was experiencing trouble breathing as my mind raced with images that were nothing more than brutal scenes from the darkest depths of my imagination. The words Six had said to me rang in my ears, over and over again like a skipping record, stuck on the worst part of the album. I wanted revenge. I looked at her, curled up on the floor, leaning against the couch, broken, sad, unsure of what was going to happen between her and I, unsure of what was going to happen between her and "the kids." I leaned down and gently placed my hand against her cheek. Her eyes were a magical blue, filled with sorrow and regret. Burning with questions on what would have happened if she hadn't decided to go out dancing that night. She was blaming herself for everything that had happened, when there was only one person in the world that needed to be blamed. She needed to stop punishing herself and inflicting the pain on herself she was inducing inside her brain, she needed to see that someone in this world wasn't here to hurt her, but instead was here to protect her from any and everything out there that ever caused her harm. I walked into my bedroom and grabbed the baseball bat that hung on my wall, signed by my favorite player, I walked back out into the living room where she was seated, crying. She looked up at me with terror in her blue eyes, unsure of what I was going to do with the bat I held so menacingly in my hands. I reached out, and took her by the hand, leading her outside to my car.

"You don't have to do this," she said. "This isn't what I want."

She said those words, but they rang with vacuous meaning. She wanted this almost as much as I wanted this. I was unwilling to allow anyone to hurt her again. I had vowed to protect her, and I had failed at that vow. Now I was going to exact my revenge on the person who had made her feel anything other than safe. She was not going to be hurt by anyone ever again, and I was going to show everyone who had ever thought about hurting her what their punishment would be.

I opened her car door and let her in the passenger side, walking around and getting in the driver seat, tossing the baseball bat in the back seat. I looked at her. Her eyes were filled with terror, fear, admiration, and love. I threw the car in reverse and backed out of my driveway. I drove through the Nashville night. I hadn't ever been to his house, but somehow I knew where I was going. It was as though she was giving me directions without saying a word. I knew my actions may have negative consequences but so were the actions of this coward. He should be punished for what he had done to not only her, but also all of the others who were living inside of her. These were the people I loved with all of my heart, and it was my duty to protect them from the actions of evil people in the world. People who had no regard for the weak. People who couldn't rely on their own intelligence. People who didn't deserve to share the oxygen with someone as wonderful as she was. His punishment was going to be a testimony to anyone who had ever harmed her throughout her life, and a message to anyone who ever thought about harming her in the future, that if anyone made her cry, I would be there to be sure they cried also.

"It's up here," she said. "On the right."

I sped up to the house, slamming on the brakes in front of Angelo's house, parking on the too skinny Nashville side streets. I got out of the car, grabbed the baseball bat from the back seat and started walking toward the house. She got out of the passenger side, and started to follow. I turned around and looked at her, shaking my head. She was not going to want to see what was going to happen in this house, on this night. She had seen too much already. She wasn't going to need these images in her head also.

Angelo lived in a shitty part of Nashville. An area, I was pleased with the fact of, that wouldn't call the police over a disturbance. They didn't want to draw more attention to their streets. What they were doing behind their closed doors were enough secrets for them. They didn't need the police coming into the neighborhood and finding out what potentially illegal, immoral, or unethical actions or supplies were being hidden from the authorities by the unspoken bond of the cultural trash of our home city. Nobody would be bothering me as I avenged the actions that had been set forth the night prior. He may not know who I am, but he would always remember my face, and her as the last time he would ever harm anyone in the way he had harmed her, and taken something from her no one would ever be able to give back.

I walked up to the cheap yellowing door with fervor and placed my booted foot against the deadbolt with every ounce of strength I had. The door jam shattered with an audible bang as splinters flew through the air littering the living room with the tiny wooden shards. Angelo, who had previously been sitting on the couch playing a video game, jumped into the air, surprised by the forced entry.

"What the fuck?" he yelled, spinning around to see who had just entered his home in one of the most illegal and egregious ways possible.

I swung the 34-inch bat with all my might, recalling every batting practice I was forced to go through as a child, making sure my form was ever so perfect in order to get the most amount of power from my swing, connecting with his side, feeling his ribs disintegrate as the bat slowed slightly as I pushed the bat through the bones beneath his skin and attempted to puncture his lung with one of the cracked calcium filled fragments now floating around inside of him. His body crumbled to the floor as I followed through with a swing that would have undoubtedly earned a "good cut" compliment from my third base coach in little league. I smiled a little as I remembered the positive reinforcements my coaches gave me.

Even though I was never able to hit lefty when I was playing baseball, the back swing on this night seemed exceptionally natural as my arms pulled in the opposite direction, the lack of power from swinging from the other side of the plate made the next contact less powerful, but being that it was against his right temple, instead of his side, he crumbled to the floor. He hit the ground with an audible thud, as a groan left his mouth. I kicked his already shattered ribs with all I had. Over and over again, my foot landed on his progressively breaking body, until I heard him scream out in pain. He attempted to guard himself against the onslaught of agony I felt he deserved, but there was no stopping his discomfort. I was not going to allow this man to ever hurt another human being again. I dropped the bat and climbed over top of him, pummeling my fists into his face. He was now unable to protect himself from the onslaught of punches being rained down upon him, and with every new blow, blood sprayed across his already disgustingly dirty Guido like apartment.

"Why?" he cried out as I continued to land blow after blow, feeling the cartilage in his nose crumble under the power of my hands, listening to the sound of his bones breaking with every punch to his now disfigured face. Blood dripped from my knuckles, and I was unsure of how much of it was his blood and how much of it was mine. It fell like a blood-red waterfall of vengeance.

"I don't deserve this," he yelled, and I stopped punching him, for a moment to catch my breath. His olive complexioned skin was now black and blue, covered with a red mark of flowing blood. His already misshaped face was swelling making him look more cave man like than he had earlier. His tangled, frizzy, mop of dark hair wad soaked up all of the blood as though it were a sponge cleaning up a spill on the living room floor. He gasped for breath, and a spattering of blood left his crooked mouth as he gagged on his own blood.

I took a deep breath and looked around the room. It had been destroyed in the mêlée. Tables had been overturned; chairs had been broken when I had first crashed into the room. I had lost my vision in that moment, and all I could see was the opportunity to teach this piece of shit the lesson he deserved. I looked to the broken down doorway, and to my horror, she was standing there in the entryway, hands covering her mouth in shock, but I could feel the respect she was also feeling for me, and how glad she was, now that she had someone in her life who would be there to protect her from all of the dangers in the world.

"Why?" he asked again.

I grabbed him by the back of his hair and pointed his face toward the entryway. He inhaled deeply, terrified by the fact he had brought this punishment upon himself, choking more on the blood that was flowing into his mouth from the broken skin and teeth I had just recently supplied him with.

"I'm sorry," he sputtered, as I turned his face away from her and back toward me. I held his head steady with my left hand, as I pulled back with my right, ready to land the last blow to his pathetic, miserable, cowardly life. I started to swing but I couldn't, something had stopped me. I turned to see, and I was looking into her beautiful blue eyes.

"No," she said, gently holding my hand. "We don't have to do this."

I looked back down at Angelo below me, and shook my head. I wanted him dead. I wanted him to never be able to do this to another person ever again. I hoped he realized I would find him and do worse than this if he ever touched someone in that way again. I slammed the back of his head into the old, worn, hardwood floor and felt his body go limp from the blow as he fell unconscious. I stood up, grabbed my bat from the floor and walked outside. A few neighbors had exited their houses and were standing on their front lawns, curious as to what was causing the disturbance in their neighborhood. I nodded to them, alerting them everything was over, and nobody cared what they were doing inside their houses. She grabbed my blood-covered hand with hers and proudly walked back with me to the car.

"Thank you," she said, over and over again. I assumed this was the first time anyone had wanted, or actually went out of his or her way, to protect her.

42

She and I stayed on the couch for a few days after that night. It wasn't the easiest thing in the world with which to cope. I had never in my life felt a rush like the one I had felt as I was taking the baseball bat to the head of the date-raping prick. It was a mixture of fear, satisfaction, power, and a complete lack of self-control all at once, rolled into a fist full of bravery. She didn't speak much after the incident, as she called it. I thought referring to it as an "incident" trivialized the situation and didn't put the right amount of blame where it truly belonged. In the hands of all of those who had hurt her over the years, not just in the hands of Angelo, but in all of the hands of all of the people who had helped turn her into the woman with whom I was in love. I had found a new level of self-worth because of what had happened; I now knew I was someone who would be able to rise up to the occasion. Many people go through life wondering if they would be able to stand up for someone they cared about, or not. I now had the burden of wonder lifted from my shoulders as to whether or not I would be a person who would be able to commit such an act on another human, no matter how deserving he was of the abuse. No matter what, throughout the rest of my life, even if I was never faced with another situation where I would have to stand up for someone I cared about, I would know in my heart of hearts that I would with little guilt about the entire matter.

She was distant now, though. She was always the talkative one out of the two of us, and now neither one of us really ever spoke, to each other, at least. We would sit in silence, waiting for the night to come so we could go to bed, the only sound filling the void between us coming from the television, which we never turned off anymore. Instead, we sat next to each other, rarely touching, just existing in the same space, so in tuned with the other's needs that even changing the channel was done in a unified front against annoying insurance commercials, and anything that may remind us of that night. That terrible night I will never be able to forget. That night where I felt a man's ribcage crumble under the force of my baseball bat. That night where I felt a face cave in from the impact of my fist. That night where I knew I would do anything to make sure she was safe. That night where I knew I had found someone I loved with all of my heart, and all of my being. That night.

She had stopped going to work after that night. I'm not sure if she felt as though people would talk about what had happened to her, or to him, and she was ashamed of what happened. Or maybe she was afraid she couldn't trust herself around the people at work and she didn't want to put herself in another position where the same sort of result ended up happening. All I knew was in the meantime we sat in silence until we knew what to say to each other besides the typical words used to fill the silence between us. The "I love you's" were used in the same way people who lacked public speaking skills used the sounds "um" and "uh." They had ceased to be real words, and instead were syllables being passed between the two of us, hoping we would one day mean them in the same way we had previously. I knew better than to hope for this outcome, but was still too reliant upon the new emotions to be ready to give up on them yet. I was afraid of what would happen to me if I had to deal with the fresh and abusive feelings of one's first real break-up. Which as a man who was 33, almost 34, I should have experienced these feelings prior, and should be more prepared to deal with them now.

I wanted to make it better between us, but I knew nothing other than time would heal the wounds. Time, however, was a fickle lover who only worked on her own schedule, and that schedule was always lacking in the necessity of the individual — specifically speaking — her and myself. Even though I had been the one to show up as the proverbial white knight to save the day, and even though I had made it a point as to never touch her in any way that could be construed as inappropriate, or unwanted, the fact that I was male was more than enough for her to have ill-will toward me. I knew she didn't blame me for anything that happened per se, but I was of the gender that had done this to her. I was part of the human race, which was the race that raised these men, that had failed to teach them not to do these things, that had been unsuccessful in instilling simple values of right and wrong in them, and that meant, in her eyes, I was as much of the problem as any one else. I accepted this as a passing phase, because even though the words were spoken as filler to stop the deafening silence hanging in the space between us, I still could hear the sincerity in her voice, and knew that with whatever feelings she hadn't yet successfully shut off inside her she spoke those words to me.

I love you.

I love you!

I love you?

I love you…

I love you.

Eight letters. Three words. One constantly changing punctuation mark. Even she wasn't sure about the validity of her statements, but she knew in her fucked up world of questions and uncertainty there was one constant; her undeniable love for me. With every question about the world around her, and how it could possibly be true that so many bad people existed, and somehow were magnetically drawn to her, as though she was the universe's punching bag, she knew she could look into my eyes and see some semblance of consistency, and goodness. While she may have confused gratitude and surprise for love, in the beginning, she now knew no other way to tell me, or anyone else for that matter, how she felt. It was just easy to repeat the same words over and over again, hoping they are reciprocated by the person to whom you are saying them.

I love you.

I love you!

I love you?

I love you…

I love you.

As distant as she seemed to be in person I knew she was trying to pull too far away for fear of what that would do to our dynamic, our relationship, our lives. It was understandable to be withdrawn and complacent after dealing with something as traumatic as that occurring in your life. The secret was not to give up on those around you who truly care and want to be there for you in your time of need. Those are the people you should hold on to for all of eternity. The people with no hidden agenda. The people with no ulterior motives. The people who will be there the next morning. They are also few and far between. So when you find them, hold on to them, and let them know how much they are cherished, because one day they may not be there anymore and you will be left alone, in the dark, wishing there was someone around just to hear you breathing.

43

"I never really thanked you," she said, looking up at me with her blue eyes sparkling in the artificial light from the lamps situated around the room. "I've never had someone there for me the way you were there that day, and I don't know if I can ever truly thank you enough. You are truly an amazing part of my life, and I don't know what I would have done without you."

I smiled as I gently stroked her soft cheek. There was something amazing that occurred when I defended her honor that night. I found a purpose in life I had never experienced before. For once in my life, based on actions I performed, I felt whole. The feeling of truly caring for someone enough to take a baseball bat to a person's chest, causing their ribs to crumble, made me realize I wasn't on this earth to sit quietly in the background. I had been wasting away in a world where nobody would ever see me, and thanks to her I knew now I would be able to face all of the trials the world would throw at me. The dangers of the world were there for lesser people to fear. I knew I would be able to stand up to the problems facing me, or those I cared about, assuming there would be people in the world, other than her, I found to care about. When I hit Angelo with the bat, and then went on to repeatedly pummel his face with my fists, I was released of the fear and the trepidation I had been dealing with my entire life. I felt as though I could do anything in this world. I could fly from the tops of rooftops. I could break the sound barrier just by running. I could do anything I wanted now, and there was nothing in the world to hold me back.

For this I had her to thank. Over the course of our relationship which had started sometime after my 33rd birthday, but well before my 34th, I had been through more than I could have ever possibly imagined, especially for the first, and potentially last relationship I would ever be in. If she hadn't come into my life I would still be the same shy, lonely guy, sitting at the bar, drinking bud lights, watching SportsCenter, and waiting for the day when I would take my last breath and finally find out if the gamble I took on being an atheist was a good one. She was the reason I no longer lived with fear. Fear of success. Fear of failure. Fear of wondering. Fear of reality. Fear of the make-believe. Fear of believing. Fear of not believing. Fear of freedom. Fear of incarceration. Fear of complacency. Fear of fear. Just fear.

While she and I sat on the couch together, I thanked her, in the only way I knew how. The way she had taught me to thank her. The way she wanted me to thank her. It was genuine, and sincere, and real, and true, and something I shared only with her, the woman I had been lucky enough to meet and fall in love with. The amount of luck I had experienced in my life before could have fit onto the head of a pin, where 10,000 times 10,000 angels danced with all of the freedom and joy their god allowed them to experience.

Thanks to her and all I had experienced due to her involvement in my life I now had more luck than ever before. She had freed me in the simplest of terms. For this I thanked her repeatedly, letting her know how much I love her. Much like she only knew how to show her affection, and feelings for me by repeating those three words, I knew how to show her my affection and feeling by doing what I would do for her now, later, tonight, tomorrow, and anytime in the future she would ever desire my services. From here until she no longer wanted me to by her side, I would thank her, in the purest way I knew how, with all my heart, and all my soul — if souls truly existed.

44

She awoke early and left immediately to go to her emergency appointment with the good Dr. Hager-Allen. Something was amiss. I could feel it throughout my entire day, from the moment I woke up to see her spot in the bed empty. Nothing more than a warm dent in the spot she normally slept. I placed my hand where she normally was found sleeping long after I ever woke, and wished she had been there, at least so I could see her wake one more time. Throughout all of time and history I relied on two things consistently to get through the days: lies I told myself and hope. Today I would be relying on both of those more than I ever had before. Apparently even though she had taught me not to fear anything, I still feared one thing — being left by her. I had to escape the house and get to somewhere I could be free to think and not be stuck in doors with only the voices in my head guiding me in my future. I threw on a pair of pants, and a t-shirt I found on my floor. Found my car keys in the pair of shorts I had worn the day before, and I left. I wasn't sure where I was going, I just knew I had to leave in that moment and go be around people, and things, and nature, and just be anywhere except for where I was sitting at that moment, in that instant.

I pulled out of my driveway in the bad, but not worst, part of town and started to drive. I didn't know exactly where I was going, but I knew I just needed to drive. Take an opportunity to clear my head, think about the world around me. Have some time to myself away from the day-to-day dealings of the world. I turned up the radio, rolled down the windows, and pushed on the gas pedal as the Tennessee air whipped, and swirled around the inside of the car, escaping out the other side, taking with it every thought released from my head in the time it was trapped within the four doors keeping me safe from all of the outside elements. Inside my metal cocoon I was safe from the wind, the rain, the snow, the heat, the cold, the cars, the trucks, the bugs, the world, but not myself and everything running through my mind. I drove, and drove, and drove until I couldn't drive anymore, never leaving the city, while never stopping anywhere until I saw my gas light come on and, like an alcoholic who had one too many in his time, life made me stop against my will.

I found myself next to the park where I used to go, long ago, whenever I needed to think. Whether it was fate, or my subconscious that brought me here, I felt a bit relieved to be where I could sit, in relative solitude, and not have to worry about seeing anyone, or not seeing anyone, who may disrupt my thought process. I walked through the sun drenched fields of the park, circling the ponds, the pavilion, the Parthenon, waiting for clarity. My head felt jumbled, confused, lost. I didn't know what I was thinking about, because I wasn't thinking about anything, and everything all at once. I was reminded briefly of one of my youthful encounters experimenting with cocaine. I remembered the rush of endorphins shocking my brain with a flood of thoughts, none of which were connected, nor were they separate. They were like individual snow flakes. Each one original and completely unique, but all of them part of one conglomerate of a problem, wanting to be solved, but wanting to exist on forever. Because people aren't the only beings in the world who are afraid of dying.

A group of young adults, aging from their early twenties, to their mid-thirties, were involved in a game of Ultimate Frisbee. I watched as they performed the sport like a ballet, throwing the disc with fluid-like motion, jumping to grasp it out of the air, out of the reach of the defender, with an end goal of landing in the end zone softly, disc in hand, to the tune of Handel's Water Music playing in my head. I wished I could play with them, but I was too involved in my own head to even think about playing any sort of sport in which I would have to run, jump, throw and catch, in some cases simultaneously.

I watched a group of fraternity brothers playing a game of soccer. They kicked the black and white checkered ball back and forth between them, talking about the party they went to the night before, and the girls they bagged, and the drinks they drank, and how much water and Gatorade it took today to make them feel human again. I wondered how much of their lack of feeling came from too much alcohol, and how much of it had to do with actions they performed while drinking too much. They laughed and threw each other high-fives while planning tonight's conquests and schedule. What sorority would they be drinking with tonight? Whatever one still trusted them enough to be seen in public with them was the answer.

I thought about my college years and remembered all the times when nothing seemed to matter. I immaturely thought my youth was behind me, and I was officially a grown up now. Now, as a 33, almost 34-year old, I saw the error in my thoughts, because there were years, upon years, upon years ahead of me where I would still be alive, and every moment alive is an opportunity to make a difference, and if you are successful in making that difference there are years upon years, after you leave this earth for whatever etherial plane you chose to believe in, where you are remembered for all of the changes you made in your time on earth. Even if you are remembered by only a handful of people a legacy has the opportunity to live on, which means my squandered years of youth, both pre and post college have been wasted in futile attempts to make absolutely no mark on this world. Thanks to her, there would be one person to remember me after I pass on. She would tell her story to her friends, and in groups of the guy who she once loved that was willing to to go to every length to make sure she was protected, and she was safe, and her honor was vindicated. Her friends would tell the story, and the story would spread and pass along from mouth to mouth, ear to ear, and I would become a folk hero in the simplest of terms. I wouldn't become a John Henry, or a Paul Bunyan, or a David, but I too would be remembered by people for a long time to come. For that I was thankful. For that I was.

Somewhere in the distance I heard a baby start to cry, in need of a mother's love, or her milk, I had never been able to discern between the two, and I wondered if I would ever have one of my own. I knew the answer, but I was a fantasizer. I had lived so long in a world of make-believe and now in this moment, faced with my own mortality, afraid of what was going to happen the next time I opened my eyes, I wanted so much more from my life. Wasted. Completely wasted. Like so many experiences I missed out on because I was too afraid to see what life was really about, I had wasted every minute of a life that at one point, potentially, held promise and hope for a future. Now there was nothing but hope, but hope, as discussed previously, was the emotion of the devil, if the devil actually existed. Apathy was the best answer to a life worth living. One who survives in apathetic fashion never gets let down, and those who get let down were never truly apathetic. There I sat, on the steps of the Parthenon, watching, observing, wishing for excitement I could control, but to want control is to want power and power has the ability to bastardize the goodness and purity of a life. My endeavors into my world was my futile attempt to control that which cannot be controlled. Slowly I was learning that fact. Slowly I saw there was no order, or fairness. There was randomness, and improbability. Life was random. Life makes little sense. To want control over these random electronic firing of synapses, would be like asking for control of the tides, or the seasons, or the rain, and no matter what Charles Hatfield insisted, nobody can control the rain.

45

I walked from the Parthenon, across the plush, green grass, over the bridge, across the pond, past one parking lot, down the trail to the second parking lot where my car was parked. Oddly, I thought about Ekow, my cab driver from the airport on multiple occasions when I seemed to be working more than I had in quite some time. I wondered if he had ever truly existed, and then wondered if any of this truly existed or if somewhere in the depths of my mind I created this world, like I created so many others to get me through the hard parts of my life, much as she created the kids to help her with situations in her life she was not emotionally or mentally prepared to cope. Reality was a matter of perception, I had read once in a story, the question was whose perception dictated whose reality?

I turned my engine on and started at the Tennessee sky that stretched out eternally in every direction. As far as one could see there was blue, like her eyes, not like the eyes of Sixteen, and not like my eyes, but like hers. In the air hung the sent of lilacs and I could have sworn that somewhere in the distance I could feel her watching me, waiting for me, loving me. A chill went through my body as I sat there, feeling an odd amount of positive anticipation for the future for the first time *ever*. There it was again: hope. The devil's horns were in me deep, and he was threatening me with his pitchfork and trying to hold me back, and the happiness hope conjures kept bringing me back. Like the wish of all lottery winners who spend their earnings on prayer after prayer that they may never have to work again after this Tuesday or Friday night. I didn't care though. I liked the feeling of hope pulsating through my body, freeing me of the burden of tragedy and anger, and disappointment. In that moment I closed my eyes and didn't imagine a world that was not my own, but the world I was in, right then, right there and I smiled, a real smile, for the first time in longer than I could remember.

I pulled my drive shaft into the reverse position and backed out of the spot, ready to head home and face the future. I knew she and I were going to be ok. There would be nothing in the world that would ever truly break the bond she and I shared. Through darkness and rain, through happiness and joy, the two of us would bond and grow and be together until the world exploded from too much love emanating from somewhere deep inside the two of us, grabbing hold of the world, like AIDS in the 80's, and changing the face of the future forever.

As I drove from the park, back into the bad part, but not the worst part, of town, I felt myself breathing easier and easier. Like a former smoker who had gone days without a cigarette, my lungs opened up, and oxygen flooded my lungs filling me with a sense of euphoria and grand happiness. There was nothing in the world that could take me down from this high. No heroin, cocaine, marijuana, DMT, acid, ecstasy, ketamine, GHB, or mescaline could produce the same sort of joy I was feeling then, in that second. I knew I would have to grab hold of it, remember it forever, remember the song on the radio, remember the scent in the air, because those moments were fleeting and they were the ones completely worth remembering. To forget those moments are the saddest losses one can experience if they would ever remember what it was to feel the way they did in that instance.

I pulled into my driveway, and I could see she was already there. I already knew what was happening when I walked in the house. She would be sitting on the pale olive green couch, waiting patiently for me to get home. She would want to tell me about her visit with Dr. Hager-Allen. She would look me in the eye and a smile would cross her face. Her smile would become infectious as we would embrace and make sweet love on that couch, before moving to the bedroom where we would do it again, and again, and again, all night long until the sun came up and I needed to rehydrate.

46

I walked into the front door of my house which was safe enough for a single man to be living in by himself, but not one safe enough for a woman to live in at all, by herself, or with anyone else. I walked past my bedroom, into the living room and there I saw her sitting on my couch. A smile crossed my face as I looked into her deep blue eyes. The smell of lilacs filled the room. If I had been paying closer attention I would have seen her eyes were filled with tears. Tears of fear. Tears of sadness. Tears of unbridled sorrow. She knew what she had to do. She had to kill me. Just as the good doctor had instructed so long ago. Just like she ignored so long ago. Just as she had to do now.

47

"I'm sorry," she said. "But Dr. Hager-Allen says I can't be with you anymore. You are a danger to my sobriety, my future, my soul. I told him he was wrong, but he reminded me that anytime I needed protection, love, guidance, hope since you and I met I came to you. I tried to stay away before, but I needed you. Now, he has told me I don't have a choice. I have to end this with you, right now, today."

48

She sat there, on my pale olive green couch, looking up at me with her blue eyes. They were filled with sadness and regret. I wanted to ask what why Dr. Hager-Allen felt that way, I wanted to know what exactly she had told him, but I was too afraid to find out the answer to that question. I was afraid of what it would feel like to hear those words, those words that would undoubtedly ruin the feelings of joy and happiness I had experienced due to the fact she came into my life.

Her eyes didn't even look blue anymore. They inexplicably seemed to have shifted to a shade of dark green. I was looking into the eyes of a woman I had fallen completely and totally in love with but looking at her eyes, I could see I didn't know who she was at this moment. I looked for words, any words, to say to end the gut wrenching silence that was standing around us making my stomach feel empty and gaseous at the same time. It was the feeling of 100,000 butterflies dying simultaneously. She just lowered her head and tears started to fall. I chewed on the scar on the inside of my lip furiously, cutting it open, tasting the blood that poured into my mouth and realizing that soon I would have a completely different scar in the same spot I would chew on in the future whenever I was feeling nervous or anxious. I didn't need to hear her say anything. I knew every word that was going to be leaving her mouth and every explanation of how she would be able to potentially justify her actions, all of them based on a single lie which she would hope be able to allow me to forgive her. A lie that consisted of three words. The most important lie we tell to people every day. She lifted her head and through the tears that fell from her newly greened eyes she said this lie, "I love you," and I could tell she was lying.

My legs didn't grow weak, they broke in that instant. It felt as though someone had hit both of my knees with a golf club as they buckled underneath me. I grabbed my balance and eased myself into the chair next to where she was sitting. My head was spinning. I knew anything I could say at that moment would be nothing more than irrational statements. I wanted to yell at her. I wanted to scream. I wanted the burning sensation that had just started permeating its way through my chest to suddenly halt and make it easier for me to breath, because at that moment the overly organic action of breathing seemed like an action I was learning how to do for the very first time. My throat felt like it was closing up, and I was unable to make any sort of sound much less a word to tell her how I was feeling. My hands were shaking. There was a throbbing in my head. I felt dizzy. The only thing I was attempting to accomplish was to not cry in front of her. I wanted her to leave so I could break down properly.

"I'm sorry," she said.

She knelt down in front me, tears falling from her eyes, but I didn't believe them. After everything I had endured, everything I had put up with, everything she had done since we met, I couldn't believe her anymore. The trust we shared was hinging on one thing, one solitary action that neither one of us was ever supposed to do. I could tell by looking at her she had done that one thing. I mouthed the word "No" and shook my head.

"I love you," she said. "From the bottom of my fucking heart, I love you. I didn't want to hurt you. I never intended for this to happen to us. I didn't know we would become what we became."

The lump in my throat was growing exponentially larger by the second. It felt as though it could be viewed by anyone in the outside world, even though rational thought told me it only felt that way because I wasn't letting it out. The pressure started to build up behind my eyes, which were still blue, and I started to feel the beginnings of tears well up in my ducts, slightly blurring my vision. I didn't want to blink for fear she would see them fall. I didn't want to show more weakness than I already had.

"You are the safest person in my life," she said. "I never wanted to hurt you. I just became too dependent on you, and I reacted negatively. It is how I push people away. I am sorry. I am so sorry. You were never supposed to be there for me."

I shook my head. It was only supposed to be a little bit of space. How did it change into this? I could feel my lip begin to quiver. My breathing had grown more intense. While it was all I could do to grab a breath a second ago, it seemed as it was the only thing I was able to do to keep myself from completely breaking down. The solitary life I had been leading up to the point of meeting her may not have had a lot of benefits, but not having this feeling pulsating through my body was one of them. I looked at this girl, who only a day before I was completely and totally in love with and wanted to curse her. I wanted to curse her for what she had done. I wanted to curse her for how she had hurt me. I wanted to curse her for making me feel the way I was feeling at that moment. I wanted to curse her for all these things, but mainly I wanted to curse her because, even though she had made me feel what I was feeling at that moment, I knew deep down I was still totally in love with her but knew I wouldn't ever be able to trust her with anything ever again.

"I warned you I would do this," she said. "I knew that I would hurt you in the end."

She had given me a gift only a few short months before, a gift I cherished more than anything else I had ever received anyone before. It was a gift that made me feel, for the first time in as long as I could recall, like a real human. Now, in that moment, she had taken that away from me. The feeling one has of truly and unequivocally loving someone who loves them back may be the one feeling worth living for. She had given me that feeling. She had taught me what it was to unconditionally love. Through everything we had experienced together, I had learned how to be accepting and how to love. Now, I had learned what most people had learned when they were teens in high school, knowing what real heartbreak felt like. The gaseous pit that was in my stomach began to grow. It slowly churned its way through my stomach, boiling up into my esophagus. The taste of bile began to surge in the back of my throat. I knew I was going to vomit.

I stood calmly. She still knelt in front of me, looking up at me waiting for any sort of response. I walked to the bathroom, to which she promptly followed.

"Why are going to the bathroom?" she asked. "What are you doing? Are you going to hurt yourself? Please, I couldn't live with it if you did something to hurt yourself"

She was filled with concern, especially as I started rushing to get there quicker, hoping I could make it before I would have to clean up a mess in my hallway on top of everything else I was going through at the moment. I knelt down in front of the toilet, yanking the seat open just as I began to throw up the contents of my stomach. I hadn't eaten in two days. All I had that morning was water. My stomach hadn't allowed for me to put anything else in it. Stress had caused me to turn myself into an anorexic mess. The painful dry heaves produced a white, medicine flavored bile that stung my taste buds and made me gag even while I was already vomiting. She sat down next to me and lightly stroked my back as I heaved over and over again. Tears uncontrollably streamed from my eyes as I attempted to purge anything from my body. Eventually the white bile changed into a brownish color, and eventually to a deep red. I saw the change in the color and I was concerned over the implications of my vomiting of blood, but I didn't mention it to her. I wasn't in need of her concern or sympathy at that moment. I had gotten everything I had needed from her a long time ago. Her hand gently rubbing my back was even too much for me to take. I wanted her out of my life forever, but I never wanted to let her go.

49

She left shortly after I finished throwing up. She told me she was sorry a few more times. She told me she loved me a few more times. She told me the lies we tell other people to soften the blows of heartbreak. The lies we tell in order to make ourselves feel better when we've destroyed the existence of another human being for our own gratification. She was gone after that. I fell back into my earlier routine I experienced when she had left for rehab. I spent a lot of time lying on my couch watching mindless television and wishing I had never met her. I wanted to talk about what I was experiencing with other people, but I had relied so heavily on her, and had actually become too dependent on her I didn't know who I would even talk about it with. I deleted her number from my phone. I deleted her from my social networking sites. I deleted her from my life. I didn't keep any of the pictures she had sent me because all they did was act as a constant reminder of how much I could love and how little I ever wanted to love someone like that again.

I went to see Dr. Hager-Allen and see if he could tell me where she was, or if she was ok. He told me she was gone, and other than that he didn't have any idea about how she was, or where she'd gone. He also said that even if he could tell me anything about her, which he couldn't due to confidentiality laws, he wouldn't be able to tell me anything about her I wouldn't already know anyway. I thought about the kids. I wondered if they would even miss me. I started to think about different conversations I had with Twelve. To think the one that I connected with the most was a 12-year old version of her. I felt bad for Six too; who did one time say I was the only man they could ever trust. I figured Sixteen wouldn't miss me too much though. Sixteen never seemed like one to care about who was around and who wasn't. Sixteen always tried to keep people at arms distance. Maybe it was Sixteen who did the act to finally push me away. Maybe it was one of the personalities I never interacted with. Maybe it was just her the entire time and I was just a pawn in some weird game she was playing. She could have told me the truth about anything, and maybe using these different identities was the way she was most comfortable opening up. I never judged her for anything. I didn't care about the addiction, until it became what eventually terminated our relationship. I didn't care about the lack of a physical relationship. I didn't care about the multiple identities living inside of her. I cared about her, and I had fallen in love with every single identity that was a part of her, because they were exactly that, a part of her. And I had fallen in love with her as a whole. I found it odd that I had somehow forged relationships with different people all rolled within one person, and how I was going to miss each one differently.

She was gone from my life. I was gone from hers. As much I wanted to be able to protect her from anything in the world that could potentially hurt her, I knew it was best for both of us to just keep our distance from each other. She needed to figure out how to protect herself. I needed to not be so dependent on protecting her. It was the only thing in my life that had ever made me feel worthwhile, but it was debilitating in its own right as well. I knew she thought about me from time to time, almost as often as I thought about her. She missed me and wished I could be there to talk to her on those nights when it seemed her ghosts didn't want her to sleep well and she just wanted someone to hold her close as she rested her head in my shoulder and told me my arms made her feel safe. I missed those moments too. I wished we could have had at least one more before we had parted ways. I missed her smell of lavender and cloves. I missed the feel of her breath against my skin. I missed her soft lips on my neck. I missed her embrace, and the tears she would cry when we reached orgasm together. I missed knowing what it was like to love someone the way I was in love with her.

Time continued to pass, and each passing day I started to find myself reverting back to my old life. I found myself occasionally going to bars again, and staring up at the televisions posted high above my head as ESPN would play the top ten plays of the day. I would drink my Bud Lights and clandestinely listen to conversations so I could hear a secret that would allow me to make up a story in my head and I would judge the person whose secret I heard all based on the story I made up for them. Nothing seemed as exciting as her story though. Hers was a story so fantastical and unbelievable I was basically unable to come up with anything as amazing in my head anymore. The world of fiction I had previously thrived in had been beaten by my own reality and with this came the moment I had to take a long hard look at my life and realize I was unable to continue to live in the fashion I had grown accustomed to. Knowing her had completely changed me to the core. I saw the world differently than I did only months before. Sometime after my 33rd birthday and before my 34th I had learned that life isn't something to be spent sitting at bars and making up stories in order to make you feel better about the banality of your life.

No, life is meant to be experienced and lived. It is meant to be taken seriously. It is meant to prove your ability to be a hero. It is time meant to be used proving your worth to the world. I found that for a few short months in my 33rd year of living that I could be someone's rock. I could be their support beam. I could be the person they lean on. It was due to the feeling of being needed that I felt important during that time period. I was there to keep her safe during her trying times. Once she realized she didn't need me anymore, she pushed me away in the only way she knew how. I couldn't really blame her for that. I wouldn't have known how to end it if I had ever decided to make that decision for the two of us. Perhaps I would have gone about it in a similar situation. Always regretting my actions of hurting her, while knowing it was best I let her go.

I was forced to look at life differently. I could see the importance of it all now. Not only in the living it properly, and to a higher standard than what I was doing before she came around, but also the fact there are true monsters in the world who only hurt others. There is a social responsibility in protecting others from the monsters that roam the world in disguise of people we should respect. They are everywhere in the world, waiting to break the trust of a poor little girl who has no way of defending herself from the people in her life she is supposed to be able to run to in a time of need. Life shouldn't have to be lived in fear, but once it is, it is comforting to know somewhere out there someone is willing to be there to protect you from all of the darkness that plagues the earth. That is my place in this world. I understand that now. While others have been put here to hurt and injure and frighten, I have been placed here to protect those they affect. Sometime after my 33rd birthday, and sometime before my 34th, she showed me my place in this world. I wish I could properly thank her for that, but I don't know if she and I will ever speak again.

The time I spent watching ESPN and drinking Bud Lights at bars could be better spent doing a myriad of other things. None of these things would be achieved as long as I sat idly by as the world passed me at 1,000 miles an hour on a daily basis.

I sipped my Bud Light and looked up at the TV, which was showing ESPN. I looked away from the glowing screen and looked down to my right. There was a girl with light green eyes, almost white, wearing a blue skirt, and a white top. She looked back at me and smiled. I smiled back.

"Hi," she said.

I laughed a little internally as I realized that now, as I was tired of being Thirty-Three, I had freedom for the first time in my life. I was no longer burdened by fear or hope or the make believe. I was there in that moment, at that time, talking to this girl in that bar for the first time ever, and I was faced with the choice of talking to her, or walking away because nothing was dictating I had to say anything, or leave that spot, or stay there, or be anywhere for that matter. I was free in the simplest of terms, and nothing could have made me want to feel anything differently about my life in that moment.

I chewed on the inside of my lip, as I tended to do from time to time, looking at those hypnotizing eyes, I said, "Can you keep a secret?"